SO SHALL THE TREE GROW

Cornbread Mafia Book Four

NINIE HAMMON

STERLING & STONE

SO SHALL THE TREE GROW

Chapter One

April 1, 2022

"MY PRECIOUS RUTHIE, *if you're reading this, it means I'm not around anymore to take care of you. So you need to know about the Tree House.*"

FORTY-TWO-YEAR-OLD RUTH HANNACKER'S legs collapsed out from under her and she made some sound, some kind of grunt as the punched-in-the-gut feeling dropped her onto the edge of the bed. Her eyes filled so suddenly with tears that the words swam on the page like she was reading them through a fishbowl.

Her mother's handwriting was square, bold, straight-forward. Mom had shown her the letters her first husband, Davie Monaghan, had written when he was in Vietnam. Well, *parts* of the letters he'd written. The man's hand-writing had looked like calligraphy. Mom told her that his handwriting on the note he'd slipped to her in American history class when they were high school seniors had so startled her she thought he must have gotten some girl to write it for him.

Jessica Harrington had gone out with him that first time because she was curious. What kind of seventeen-year-old boy had handwriting that looked like art?

Mom's handwriting was as no-nonsense as she was.

Ruth's eyes shifted to the date on the top of the letter she held in now-trembling hands — July 9, 1988. She instantly connected the dots. That was *the year.* The year Mom had been in a car wreck. It'd been more than just a fender-bender; the car had rolled. Her arm had been broken in two places, she had a six-inch gash on the side of her head and her whole body'd been bruised like — her words, "like I'd been inside one of those drums they use to tumble Bingo numbers."

When Ruth was older, she figured out that the experience had forced her mother to face her own mortality, and Jessica Monaghan must have decided there were loose ends in her life she didn't want to leave dangling. That decision had been a watershed event in the lives of nine-year-old Ruth and eighteen-year-old Drew Hannacker. In Sherry Lynn Hannacker's life, too.

Jessica sat Ruth down and told her the identity of her father — that mythical man her mother'd refused to talk about, except to say that he loved them both and would be with them if he could. Ruth remembered how shocked she'd been to find out her father was *Riley Hannacker* — shocked, but not really surprised. A lot of things made sense then — including their twice-a-month treks to the federal prison in Beckley, West Virginia, four and a half hours away — how the trips were *sacred,* nothing kept her mother from going.

Her mother'd talked to Drew, too ... and to Sherry

Lynn Hannacker — irrevocably changing the lives of all three of them. Now, as Ruth looked down at the letter in her hands, she realized that among the loose ends her mother'd felt the need to tie up was writing a letter to her only daughter to tell her a secret. It was literally a "secret from the grave," whispering into Ruth's ear three months after Jessica had died in the devastating tornado in western Kentucky right before Christmas that'd killed fifty-six people. Ruth had stumbled upon the letter when she came home for a weekend to clear out some of her mother's things — a task she had been putting off for months.

Taking a deep, calming breath, Ruth wiped the tears off her cheeks, forced herself to continue reading the words on the sheets of stationery she'd found at the bottom of her mother's jewelry box. She'd spotted the box in the back of the attic, out-of-sight out-of-mind for who knew how long behind a box of Christmas decorations and the Nativity set with the broken Baby Jesus Ruth hadn't seen since she was a little girl. Blowing the dust off the box, Ruth had started to go through it, and discovered under a tangled pile of costume jewelry necklaces, a sealed envelope with the words "For Ruth" written on the outside.

"Only four people in the world — Nate and Riley Hannacker, Willie Ray Taggart and me — ever knew the Tree House existed, that it was real and not the myth Willie Ray made it out to be. The day we started digging the hole, he told us that the best way to keep the secret was to go out and tell everybody he knew about it — and so he did. He'd brag about it to anybody who'd listen, how he'd buried a propane tanker in a field and stashed inside it all the money he made growing weed. It made a great story, a tall tale, a preposterous myth. What nobody knew but the four of us was that he'd been telling the truth. Willie Ray really *did* bury a propane tanker in a field and he really *did* fill it up with money."

Ruth might actually have gasped, she couldn't tell for sure. She did know that her heart suddenly shifted into a gallop in her chest, forcing her blood through her veins in a tympani-drum rhythm she could feel in her temples. And she felt … what? *Alive!* Ruth had been stumbling through every day since her mother's death, feeling empty and numb and … dead inside. This letter — the secret it was imparting — was the first thing powerful enough to shove aside the aching pall of grief that had settled around her, hanging on like a frigid winter relentlessly resisting the warmth of spring.

Wild tales about buried boxcars and tankers full of money somewhere out in the hills were part of the wallpaper of life in Callison County. Everybody'd heard them. Oh, they weren't true, of course … but it was fun to consider the possibilities. Now, Ruth Hannacker held in her hand … it was a secret map to a pirate's treasure.

"The money in the Tree House kept you and me and a whole lot of other families afloat after the FBI seized all the Cornbread Mafia's offshore accounts in 1978 and confiscated everything the government could lay hands on that'd been purchased with funds from our 'criminal enterprise.'"

Cornbread. Mafia. If ever two words needed a trigger warning, those did.

The words rang with the resounding toll of huge cathedral bells down in the depths of Ruth Hannacker's soul. She had heard about the Cornbread Mafia her whole life. Everything in her world when she was growing up related to it in one way or another. The Cornbread Mafia was magical to her, as if her mother and the others had been members of some holy organization like the Knights Templar. Oh, it had already been crushed, ground into the dust under the jack-booted heel of the mighty Federal Bureau of Investigation before Ruth was born, but still it had formed and shaped her world and the people in it, a little community as close-knit as steel wool where a generation of men had been hauled off and put in cages for … what? Criminal farming.

Almost a hundred Callison Countians had been busted working in Cornbread Mafia fields in seven states. They'd all been tried and were sentenced according to the marijuana laws in the state where they got caught. Unfortunate men like Joe Gabis, who'd stood before a "hangin' judge" in Missouri, spent almost a decade behind bars. Most got lesser sentences. But this was Callison County, Kentucky — a place where big Catholic families raised broods of rowdy kids and lived in old farm houses with wraparound porches … or in clapboard shacks with dirt yards littered with the carcasses of dead appliances and dismembered automobiles. Brewster was a little five-traffic-light town that didn't have a McDonald's, a Walmart, a movie theatre or an open-24-hours anything. So a *hundred* families — every man, woman and child in the whole community — had a husband/father/son/brother/uncle/grandfather/boyfriend or next-door neighbor who'd been locked away for no good reason.

Oh, that'd been more than four decades ago, and the community had recovered from the original blows, but the ripple effects had cascaded down through generations. You didn't have to scratch too deep in any Callison County family to find a connection to the Cornbread Mafia, or to find its attendant loathing of federal authorities.

It had always seemed to Ruth that who she was had been defined and refined by an organization that hadn't existed since before she was born. Her mother was strong because she'd had to be to make it in post Cornbread

Mafia Callison County. Ruth had watched, listened, conformed to that image. Her mother had been resourceful — so Ruth learned to be. Her mother had been smart, clever, stayed a step ahead of whoever was coming up behind. And she never gave up. Ruth followed suit, was a fierce competitor — particularly in sports. Tall like her mother, Ruth's all-arms-and-legs six-foot frame was made for basketball and she was a star, towering over the other girls, dominating the court. She wore her butter-colored hair in a single braid all the way down her back, and her fair complexion earned her the nickname "the Ghost," who could appear out of nowhere to block opponents' shots and steal the ball. Ruth didn't just like to win, she *had* to win. It mattered. She'd learned all that at the feet of the Cornbread Mafia.

And *now* …

Now she was being entrusted with one of their secrets.

The letter described how Willie Ray had badgered the others into helping him bury a propane tanker as a place to keep his money because he refused to put it in an account on some island "he hadn't never been to." They'd called it the Tree House because Willie Ray and her father had found the limestone cave the day they'd gone into the woods to build a treehouse. Her mother set down in clear script the combination to the locks, told her to take a lantern because there was no light, and warned her that Willie Ray had only been right about secrets when you wanted to make them into myths. Real secrets were just that — secret. She must never tell anybody about the existence of the Tree House.

"Ruthie, honey, I'm giving you the Tree House because if I'm gone, you'll need those resources before your father gets home. It's there as a safety net. It's there to fund your future, way more than most young people have to set up their lives. So use it wisely and with gratitude."

Ruth lost it then, sobbed, tears flooding down her cheeks, and her shoulders shaking, though she didn't make a sound. She wept for the mother whose passing had ripped out her soul, clinging tight to the letter "For Ruth," hugging it to her chest. When she was cried out, she left the three piles she'd been sorting her mother's things into "keep," "sell" and "Goodwill" on the bed and went downstairs. If Willa had still been in the kitchen, Ruth would have shared the secret with her, but there was only a pot of beans simmering on the stove and the girl's truck was no longer parked behind the house. She'd left for her dentist appointment.

Digging around on the shelf in the hall closet, Ruth found a flashlight that actually worked. She had no idea where there might be a lantern and didn't want to take the time to go buy one. Of course, she needed to talk to her father about the Tree House, but she wanted to see it for herself, first. Gratefully, he wasn't still sitting in the rocker on the front porch — where he spent most of every day now. She could slip past while he was taking a potty break and not have to tell him where she was going.

How much money was still there now, after all these years, she wondered. Maybe there was none at all. The amount didn't matter — unless it was some humongous figure — find a couple hundred thousand bucks, that'd matter to anybody. Finding a fortune was not the motivation here, though. It was ... the mystery. The adventure. She found excited anticipation bubbling up in her chest where there had been nothing but the ragged edges of grief before and she was grateful for the brief reprieve. Grabbing a jacket off the hook by the door, she pocketed the keys to the Honda Accord parked out front that she had rented at Louisville International Airport. She wasn't completely sure where the roads her mother had described were located, but she'd figure it out. Or she'd stop and ask. She'd find the place, oh, my yes, she surely would. She wouldn't stop looking until she did.

As she drove through town, it occurred to her that there wasn't a person in sight who hadn't heard one of the tall tales about "weed money buried in a field." And now, Ruth Hannacker was about to go dig it up.

Chapter Two

Seventy-two-year-old Riley Hannacker shook his head at the cosmic irony of it all. A tornado had blown Jessica Monaghan into Riley's arms almost forty-four years ago, and three months ago, another twister had blown her right back out again.

He stepped out on the front porch as his daughter Ruth's rental car turned out of the driveway and onto the highway, and sat back down in the rocking chair he'd bought for his grandfather to replace the lawn chair where the old man's left butt cheek hung out a hole in the seat.

Rocking slowly back and forth, he looked out into the distance, the thousand-yard stare in his eyes registering nothing at all. It was too cool to be sitting out on the front porch. Most of March had been warm, but winter hadn't picked up its ball and gone home just yet.

Riley didn't care if it was cold, wasn't aware of anything except that the motion of rocking, the back and forth, back and forth of it, was soothing in a way he couldn't explain. Rocking was an external response to an internal condition. He was hollow inside. Empty. The place his heart had once been was a vacant cavern where gusts of chill wind blew through the tattered remnants of his soul. The rocking kept time with the rushes of internal cold, established a rhythm with the gusts of frigid air, a ship propelled across a stormy sea.

The first twister had come roaring over King's Crown Knob, not a very big one, really, but big enough to take the roof off the barn on Booker Road where Jessie'd been working trimming buds. Big enough to make that horrifying freight-train roar. Big enough to send her scurrying for cover under a water trough absolutely terrified. She had clung to him when he found her there, pulled her into his arms in the rain, wouldn't let her be all tough and self-sufficient and strong.

"You almost got carried away by a tornado. You're entitled to be upset about it." She had broken then, clung to him in hysterical tears, sobbing as he helped her out of her soaked clothing.

It'd just happened. Unplanned — well, except in every fantasy Riley had had about women since he was sixteen years old. And maybe planned by Jessie, too. She never said it in so many words, but she'd told him that her feelings for him had been growing for years and she hadn't known what to do with them. Not with Davie at home, lying beneath starched white sheets, staring sightlessly at the ceiling. Smiling sometimes. Drooling sometimes, too.

She'd said that when Riley had demanded that they vote — black rocks in a box — about whether or not they should kill Jackson McClusky, she'd known then that he'd done it for her. To spare her feelings. Because he'd known from personal experience that killing somebody — even if it's justified, even if it's in self-defense — changes a person. They're never the same again, and he wanted to spread the responsibility around among the three of them, to protect

Jessie from pain and remorse somewhere out there in the future when she was no longer fueled by white hot, homicidal fury. He didn't want her to see her reflection in the mirror and regret what she'd allow herself to do.

She'd seen his love then, she told him later, and had been forced then to admit that she loved him, too.

But that day after the tornado had left Jessie unharmed, as they clung to each other in the pouring rain, it hadn't been about giving in to some long pent-up passion. It could have been, but it wasn't. It really had "just happened." Neither planned it, and neither regretted it.

Well, Jessie had for a time. She wouldn't see Riley like that again, could not countenance divorcing Davie to marry him. Though when she discovered she was pregnant with Ruth, it had burned up every drop of regret, like the warm morning sunshine melts the dew off a rose.

That first storm, the power of it, had seemed to him to be a perfect metaphor for their love. Wild and fierce and strong … and unexpected. Sometimes, when he lay in his cell, listening to the clunking of the locks in the cell block after lights out he imagined that he could hear again the freight train sound of the storm, sense the pressure of it, the way it sucked all the air out of the world, inhaling like a kid about to blow out the candles on a birthday cake.

The second twister, the one that took Jessie from him, was a metaphor for nothing. It was evil incarnate. It had been a monstrous beast writhing in the darkness, hell-bent on absolute annihilation, a ravenous monster devouring everything in its path in a mindless frenzy of destruction. The biggest, meanest of *seventy-one* confirmed tornadoes in five states in the Ohio Valley, Dec. 10, 2021, it'd snared a spot in the record books as the longest, strongest tornado in U.S. history. In just under three hours, the EF 4 twister chewed up and spit out 230 miles of real estate, laying waste to woodlands, leveling the trees and stripping the bark off, sweeping away houses and towns and buildings like swiping the little green and red boxes off a Monopoly board. It tossed around road graders and fully-loaded coal trucks like Tonka toys, ripped the hide off cattle, drove fence posts through walls, stained glass through bricks, uprooted gasoline pumps and then blew out the flames of their explosions.

Smashing down on the unsuspecting out of the cold darkness, it slaughtered fifty-six people before its butchery was complete. One of those people was Jessica Ann Harrington Monaghan Hannacker.

While Riley lay unconscious in a Fort Campbell hospital, workers frantically dug through the debris searching for any sign of survivors. After two nights of below-freezing temperatures, the rescuers stopped looking for survivors and scoured the piles of rubble for bodies.

They didn't find Jessie until three days after the twister struck. Her body was wrapped up in a piece of tin stuck in the bare branches of a persimmon tree. The cadaver dogs followed the smell.

Nobody knew that she had been literally ripped out of his arms. Riley hadn't told anybody that part. He never would. All those years ago when the guard unit was activated, Riley had struggled to grasp the reality of it. Willie Ray'd come down Hunter Lane honking his horn, his face so pale his freckles stood out on his skin like sequins — "You'd best pack up your sunscreen, Riley boy," he'd said. "They're fixing to send our asses to Vietnam."

After Riley'd held a hysterical Sherry Lynn while she cried, after he'd sat on the porch with Papa staring out at nothing, after all that, Riley had gone into the bathroom, closed the door and said out loud over and over, "Vietnam. Vietnam. Vietnam." And the saying of it finally made it real, made him believe it was really happening that he was going to some jungle on the other side of the planet and shoot at people … and that they'd shoot back.

Riley hadn't told anybody about Jessie's final few moments, the freight-train sound eating up the world around them, because to say it out loud would make it real. And even now, three months later, he couldn't bear for that part to be real.

It broke his heart to think about the past, but looking back was all he had. Looking forward was a view of … nothing. Without Jessie to live by his side, what was he going to do with the remaining years of his life?

Chapter Three

The letter from her mother that now served as Ruth's treasure map had provided directions to the property where the Tree House was located along with a description of how to get from the road up the side of the knob to the pile of boulders that concealed the entrance. But the directions featured landmarks from four decades ago! How many of them even existed anymore?

Ruth should have called Willa and asked her to cancel her dentist appointment to help her look. It would have taken zero convincing to get the girl to bail on, her words: "a road crew rolling into my mouth with a wrecking ball and a jackhammer." Ruth couldn't help smiling when she thought about her cousin. The term "cousin" was not used in its strictest sense, of course, but nobody bothered to make distinctions about such things in Callison County. Ruth's father Riley Hannacker was Willa's grandfather — exactly what degree of cousin-age that made the two of them was anybody's guess. Ruth had never met Willie Ray Taggart, her father's best friend, but Papa always said being around Willa "amounted to the same thing."

God had reached deep down into the gene pool to create the offspring of Drew Hannacker and Andrea Taggart. Andrea was the daughter who had been born to Willie Ray's brother, Andy, when the National Guard unit was deployed in Vietnam. The daughter Andy never met. She hadn't inherited her father's platinum blond hair, though. In fact, it was Drew Hannacker who had hair so blond it almost looked white when it bleached out in the summertime.

Still, it had been a surprise to everybody in the family when Andrea and Drew's first child came into the world wailing with a set of lungs like the billows on a forge and a soft fuzz of bright red hair on her head. Drew and Andrea had already decided that if they had a baby girl they would name her Melissa Lynn, after Andrea's mother, Melissa and Drew's mother, Sherry Lynn. But the little redheaded baby was so ... surprising, so unique ... that the name they'd already selected didn't seem to fit. It had been Andrea who suggested that they name her Willa Rae — after all, she did favor her great uncle Willie Ray.

What shouldn't have surprised anybody was that the little redheaded girl had inherited more than hair color from her namesake. Ruth's mother, Jessie, tried to describe it often, but usually ended up just trailing off into silence. None of Ruth's generation had ever met Willie Ray, but they all felt like they knew him because Riley Hannacker talked about his best friend so often. As Willa grew older, Papa said having her around was like having Willie Ray back in his life. Which would mean that Willie Ray Taggart must have been a spark plug ... no, a blown transformer, with energy arcing and sparks flying everywhere. Willa's red hair was the color of flames leaping up off a fireplace log, and if she'd had even one more freckle, she'd have had to hold it in her hand. She was pretty but not beautiful, with a personality so engaging, people responded to that rather than her pleasing facial features.

Ruth rounded a bend and was rewarded with the sight of a "bald knob," a knob with no trees on the top — just like her mother'd described in her letter. Ruth was on the right track! She passed a house with a yard full of children and thought about what Willa'd asked her this morning — "Don't you wish you'd settled down, got married and had kids?" Ruth hadn't been surprised by the question. She was forty-two years old, never had a serious relationship, and Willa was thirty, that *what-have-I-done-with-my-life?* age, and not married either. But Willa was perilously close to an engagement ring on her finger for the first time in her life so she probably saw Ruth as the Ghost of Christmas Future if the romance went south. Ruth certainly could have been shocked by how blunt and direct and borderline rude the question was, but … that was just Willa.

"I still might," she'd said. "I'm not ready for the bone yard yet." But Ruth Hannacker had long since shaken hands with the reality that at the time in life when you made those connections, invested in those relationships, poured yourself into other people, a husband and children — she'd been working eighteen-hour days growing her business. She figured that ship had sailed.

Willa'd given her a knowing look.

That girl didn't miss much.

"Okay, I'm not deliriously happy … but I'm hardly ever sad." Ruth was a woman comfortable in her own skin, had lived her life on her terms and it had been enormously rewarding and fulfilling. She was damned proud of what she had built. *Had* built, past tense. Not much left of it anymore.

Willa'd seemed to look right through her, into her soul.

Ruth had wondered what truth the girl saw there. Then Willa'd changed the subject to the old man on the porch.

"HE STILL SITTIN' *out there?" Willa asks, gesturing to the front door beyond which her grandfather, Ruth's father, sits in a rocking chair, staring at nothing. When Ruth nods, Willa plops down in front of the fireplace, leans back, drapes her legs over the arm of the big brown chair and holds her feet close to the flames.*

Ruth had insisted on building a fire in the fireplace — for all kinds of reasons, most of which had nothing to do with the fact that it had turned seriously cold in the past week. Her mother had always loved having a fire in the hearth. Apparently, the original old farm house hadn't had one, but her mother installed one, with a big stone fireplace, for Willie Ray Taggart during the handful of years when he hung his hat on a nail by the door and called it home. He'd never purchased the property, of course — none of them had been big into deeds, contracts and the like with each other — so it had still belonged to Riley when Willie Ray died. And since Riley had inherited the farm from his grandfather, it was not subject to the forfeiture of property that had scraped all the Cornbread Mafia's ill-gotten gains off into a sack and handed it over to the feds. Sherry Lynn and Drew had moved into the farm house when they were evicted from the mansion she'd built. They only lived there a couple of years before Ruth's mother, Jessie, bought the farm from them so Sherry Lynn could move into Brewster, closer to her job as an X-ray tech at Callison County Hospital. They'd left Drew's horse, Coco, at the farm, so Drew spent every second of his spare time there. Ruth had grown up thinking of Drew as her big brother — long before she learned he really was.

"What are you grinning about?" Willa suddenly asks. Ruth didn't realize she was smiling.

"I was just trying to picture Papa and Willie Ray Taggart as children — you know, playing in the creek, or climbing trees, or getting into little-boy mischief."

"Like freckle-counting?"

Ruth's smile spreads. "Well, yeah——"

"'Cause if you think I'm gonna take my clothes off and stand outside so you can count 'em, that'd be a firm no. Full stop."

"You think Papa wanted to know how many freckles Willie Ray had or was it the other way around?"

The two are referring to the oft-repeated story of the day Nate Hannacker had found Riley in the back yard with a 'buck nekkid' Willie Ray "tryin" to count Willie Ray's freckles — outside, "so's there'd be good light."

"My money's on Grandpa." Willa makes a sweeping gesture that takes in her whole body. "They're my freckles, every last one of them, and I've never once wanted to know how many——" She pauses. "But when I was a kid, I did wonder what would happen to them when I grew up. Would I just get more freckles the older I got? Or would the freckles I already had get bigger? And if they didn't, if they stayed the same size, then would they be spaced farther and farther apart?"

"Is that what you wanted?"

"Big spaces between the freckles, you mean? A freckle here, a freckle there — God, no! I'd look like my pen exploded in my face. With the current spot distribution, I like to think of my complexion as a speckled countertop where you can't see the spills."

"In Medieval times, freckles meant you were a witch."

"Burned at the stake. Fried Willa. Make mine medium rare with a side order of onion rings."

Willa laughs. It's a musical sound. When she was little, Ruth thought it sounded like sleigh bells, heard from far off on a snowy morning. It's a contagious, engaging, happy sound that makes you want to laugh with her, to enjoy the moment as much as Willa is. And Willa Hannacker does know how to have fun. She calls it her superpower.

"Haven't you ever even wanted a rough estimate?"

Willa pauses, then lifts her wrist and speaks into her Apple watch.

"Hey Siri."

"I'm listening," says the automated un-person in a British accent.

"How many freckles do I have?"

"There is an app called Freckle Tracker you can download to your phone. Check it out."

"An app." Willa shakes her head. "Naaaa, that takes all the magic out of it."

They both fall silent, Ruth sorting through a pile of her mother's sweaters, Willa shifting her gaze from the front door to the fire.

"Mom says Dad never got over his grief after he watched his grandfather get shot, just a four-year-old," Willa says thoughtfully. "He was just a little boy and Grandpa's seventy-two. You think grief is harder on you when you're young or when you're old?"

Ruth shrugs and gets to her feet.

"I still have one bedroom upstairs to go through and the attic."

"And I have an appointment with a canister of nitrous oxide — the whole canister. I'll start a pot of beans before I leave, but Mama will have to make the cornbread when she gets here."

The whole family is gathering for supper tonight.

Both of them look toward the front door beyond which an old man sits in a rocker staring out with sightless eyes.

"Maybe the littles will pull him out of his funk," Willa says. The "littles" are the youngest two of Willa's sister Lissa's children.

Willa's and Ruth's eyes meet and they shake their heads in unison.

"Naaaaa."

IT WAS ONLY THEN that Ruth remembered the family supper set for tonight. Bad timing. How could she face the whole family if she'd just discovered Willie Ray's treasure? Or if she couldn't find it?

Chapter Four

Even locals would consider this remote corner of Callison County far up in the knobs near the Nelson County line "out in the boondocks." Ruth's mother hadn't explained in the letter what Ruth's father and Willie Ray Taggart had been doing here when the little boys had decided to play in the woods. There were few houses on McCubbin Lane, and most of those were clustered around the spot where it intersected US 68. None of the houses was old enough to have been here in the early 1960's when two ten-year-old boys had decided they were going to build a treehouse.

Ruth drove slowly, not impeding traffic since there was none. She hadn't seen another vehicle of any kind since she turned off on the lane. She was looking for a spot with a rock wall near the roadway where a slab of rock the size of a garage had let go and fallen off. The slab lay only a few feet from the road, impossible to miss — or so her mother's letter had said. At least in 1988 it had been and surely it was still there. Ruth couldn't imagine why some road crew would have identified the rock as a traffic hazard and hauled it away — not in a part of the county where the roads weren't even re-paved more than once a decade.

Still … if somebody had moved that rock …

Then she rounded a curve and spotted it lying right where it'd been when her mother first saw it, and for several thousand years before that, she supposed, though her understanding of geology was necessarily sketchy, since it hadn't been a required course at Stanford University's School of Business.

Pulling off the road next to the rock, she got out of her car and headed out on foot. Her mother had made it clear that she'd have to "find" the spot because there was no trail or path leading to it. Ruth clambered up through the trees and brush on the side of the knob toward the top, looking for the next identifying landmark.

"There is a pile of boulders at the base of the hill beside a meadow."

She'd said the two little boys had scared up a rabbit in the meadow and chased it to the pile of boulders. Climbing up on top of the rocks trying to get at the rabbit, they'd found an open area between two big rocks that you couldn't see from below. The open area led to a small cave, the secret cave Riley and Willie Ray had dubbed the Tree House. Jessie had purchased the property through some corporation and in 1975, she and Riley, Willie Ray and Nate Hannacker had spent most of the summer using a backhoe to dig a hole in the meadow, breaking through into the ceiling of the cave. Then they'd lowered Willie Ray's tanker down into the cave through the hole, and covered the whole thing back up again.

Making her way up the side of the knob, Ruth searched for the meadow, but couldn't find it. From the top of the knob, she surveyed what she could see below — no meadow. She made her way down the knob by traversing it, back and forth, and still couldn't find the meadow. But she did stumble upon a pile of boulders entangled in brambles and dead Kudzu vines next to the woods. Beside it was a new-growth forest … that'd been a meadow almost half a century ago.

She paused to catch her breath before climbing up onto the boulder pile, took off her jacket and tied the arms around her waist. Though her breathing returned to normal, her heartbeat still banged away in a staccato rhythm in her chest. Until this moment, she hadn't really believed she'd be able to find the Tree House, feared that time and nature had obscured the location so much in the past fifty years, it would be unrecognizable. But here it was. The boulders were huge and she'd have to climb through the vegetation that had grown up over them. But at forty-two, Ruth was in excellent shape, worked out regularly with a personal trainer, had run a marathon last summer.

But climbing the boulder pile was considerably harder than it'd looked like it'd be from below. Two ten-year-old boys had scuttled up them like spiders, but Ruth had to grunt and sweat and curse her way to the top of the pile, sacrificing three of her expensive acrylic fingernails in the effort. As soon as she reached the summit, the hole between the rocks that'd been invisible from below opened up before her and she dropped down into it. Right in front of her lay a crack in the rock of the hillside and a step or two into it revealed it was the opening of a cave. Her heart began to bang around in her chest like a sperm whale in a fish tank. Flipping the switch on the flashlight sent the shadows scurrying to the corners and revealed what looked like a gigantic silver egg, fit snugly into the cavern. Rockfall from above — whether planned or accidental — had buried the back portion of the propane tanker, but the doorway cut into the side was still easily accessible. The cave was a typical Kentucky limestone cave — which meant it was dry, no leaking water or moisture to cause rust.

"Riley found a vault door from a walk-in safe at an auction and helped Willie Ray weld it into the opening," her mother's letter'd said. "Safe as a bank vault."

Ruth had memorized the combination, but the knob was stiff from disuse and refused to turn at first. It grudgingly gave way after more grunting and cursing and she was able to twist the dial around and around freely. It took multiple attempts to get the numbers and letters just right, but then she heard a click from inside the door, pulled on the lever and the door opened, swung easily out on hinges as silent as if they'd recently been treated with WD-40.

Stepping inside, she breathed old air that smelled like the interior of a ship. Shelves made from two-by-twelves and concrete blocks lined the walls. Most of them were bare, but a row of closed cash boxes rested on the middle shelf across from the door, more than a dozen of them all the same — a little over twelve inches by about eight inches, and four inches deep.

She stepped up to the shelf and flipped the catch on the first box. Slowly lifting the lid, she shined the light inside. Nothing. The box was divided into six slots for bills and above those, four slots for coins. All the slots were bare.

Her heart sank. All that effort and anticipation … she'd been silly. The Tree House had clearly been a treasure trove of cash once. Years ago, there'd probably been full cash boxes on all the shelves, but it was foolish to believe there was money in it still.

Ruth opened the second box and found all six slots full of bills, *hundred-dollar bills.* She almost dropped the flashlight in surprise.

She opened the next box. Full. And the next. Full. All bills, no change.

There was money in every one of the boxes except the first. Ruth couldn't begin to estimate how much. Slots in some of the boxes held twenties instead of hundreds. At the far end of the shelf there were quart jars instead of boxes, filled with she didn't know what, but it wasn't money. There were six or seven of them, each labeled and there was a ledger book of some kind lying on the shelf beside them.

Ruth turned back to the boxes of bills. She'd left them standing open and she ran her flashlight across the line of them, the money inside leaping out of the darkness of each box as the beam passed.

She barked out a burst of sound that was somewhere between a cough and a bleat of laughter.

Boxes full of money.

Seriously!

Oh, she *had* to share this.

Pulling her phone out of her pocket, she saw she'd missed three calls. Ruth had a bad habit of turning off her ringer and forgetting to turn it back on. It was an old phone, an iPhone 7 or 8, and cranky, didn't hold a charge well and it only vibrated if it happened to be in the mood. She expected to see that she had no reception — out in the middle of nowhere, in a metal tanker in a cave — but she had bars! Let's hear it for Verizon's 5G network.

Punching favorites, then an emoji with red hair, she waited through three rings before a voice finally came on the line.

"'Lo, Ruth," Willa said. The words sounded funny. "You done sep-ratin'—?

"What are you doing?"

"Tryin' not to drool."

"Huh?"

"Mouth's numb. Wanted laughing gas, got a needle full of Novocain. On my way to—"

"Don't."

"Don't what?"

"Don't go … wherever you were going."

"Wh—?"

"Whatever you were planning to do, don't. Come here."

"And 'here' is—?"

"A cave full of buried treasure."

Chapter Five

Back and forth.

Back and forth.

The old rocker made no sound, never had, and Riley'd always wanted it to. Rocking chairs were supposed to creak, weren't they? The rocker in Willie Ray's living room when they were kids had a whole vocabulary of sounds, slaps and squeaks, but it'd been a platform rocker and those were nosier than regular rockers. He and Willie Ray'd get it going and it'd sing out, inching its way across the room with every rock.

Willie Ray. He'd been dead for four decades and yet Riley thought about him almost every day. He'd always heard that old people were like that — remembered the ancient past better than they remembered what they'd had for breakfast. Now Riley was one of them. No, not old. Jessie did *not* like the word old.

. . .

JESSIE PEERS *at Riley over the top of her rimless glasses, giving him the look she'd used to keep uncounted numbers of Callison County third-graders in line for three decades.*

"Is that what you're going to call it — a retirement home?" she asks.

He'd just hung up from talking to Drew about the house he and Jessie had just built on the shore of Kentucky Lake near Land Between the Lakes State Park in western Kentucky.

"It is a retirement home."

"No it's not. A retirement home is a house where retired people live."

"Well, yeah. If it walks like a duck …"

"But we're not retired people." She cocks her head at him. "Maybe you are, but I'm not."

"So what was all that about — turning in your chalkboard and your sweater with that stupid embroidered apple on the front, and announcing 'thirty years' worth of nine-year-olds is enough'? How is that not retiring?"

"I quit. I didn't retire."

"Sounds like a distinction without a difference to me. Why are you getting your panties all in a wad about retiring?"

"Old people retire. I'm not old."

They're seated in the rocking chairs on the front porch, looking out at a velvet black sky where the stars are as big as chunks of ice, and he reaches over and pats her knee. "Sweetie, you are the youngest sixty-five-year-old for a hundred miles in every direction."

She is, too. Riley isn't just blowing smoke. She'd been the most beautiful woman he'd ever seen the day they hauled him off to federal prison in 1979 and she still was when they released him in 1998 — with a few months knocked off his sentence for good behavior. She'd been forty-seven then and there was not a speck of gray in her crown of golden hair. She said Davie told her it was "the color of butter," and it was. But when the silver came early, it took over and she let it, didn't color it to keep it the blonde it'd been in her youth. She was rewarded for that decision — silver gave way to a cloud of purest white. It was absolutely regal. With that mane of snow-white hair — tall, slender and strong — Jessica Hannacker could be an intimidating woman when she tried to be, never had a single discipline problem in thirty years of teaching.

Riley winks at her.

"The hottest one, too. I'd pinch your ass, but I'd have to get up ... and then I'd have to bend over, and with my bad back," he emits a fake groan, "and my arthritis," he pronounces it arthur-itis, *"and the rheumatism," pronounced* rhuma-tiz, *"a'chewin' on my old bones, I ain't sure I could stand back up—"*

"Put a sock in it."

He loves the warmth in her voice. She holds up one of the needles in her admittedly gnarled fingers.

"I mean ... look at me. I'm knitting, for crying out loud. Knitting!" She'd started knitting to have something to do with her hands on the long drives back and forth from Callison County to western Kentucky, when they'd first started going there for weekend getaways. Pretty soon, she was making afghans and sweaters and scarves — even had a booth one year at the Callison County Burley Festival. "I don't feel old. I don't want to be old."

"Then don't. I don't plan to."

"I don't want that number — sixty-five — to become the hall monitor of my life. The yardstick where I measure out what I can and can't do. Skydiving? Oh, goodness no, why I'm sixty-five—"

"You wanna go skydiving?"

She gives him a withering look. "I don't want it to mean anything. It's just a number."

"And 'retirement home' — just words. They can mean whatever you want them to."

"Okay, if I get to pick, they mean 'base camp.'"

"You lost me."

"Like when you're climbing Mount Everest and every so often you

stop, you build a place and stay there for awhile before you keep climbing."

"Don't you think it'd be a more fitting analogy if we were coming down the back side of the mountain instead of climbing up the front?"

"You saying we've already been to the peak, we've gotten as high as we're ever going to go and everything from now on is downhill?"

He hears a little tremor in her voice, sets down his glass of ice tea, reaches out and takes her hand.

"This really has you spooked, doesn't it? Why?"

It isn't like any of it is a surprise. They had spent years daydreaming and fantasizing. They'd gone to Land Between the Lakes the first time when Ruth bought them a weekend package at the lodge to celebrate the ribbon-cutting on her first Ruth's Stuff boutique in Lexington. She'd said they worked too hard and needed to get away. Talk about the pot calling the kettle black! Their daughter put in eighteen-hours days, worked nights and weekends for years building her chain of "stores selling pretty things," as she called them. He and Jessie had hoped Ruth would relax after she got two locations up and running, but instead of slowing down she had doubled-down, opened two more stores before branching out into a line of antique stores called Has-Beens. After that, she traveled the country, scouring attics and yard sales and estate sales. They'd certainly gotten their money's worth from her Stanford University Business School degree. He and Jessie'd talked about where the girl's drive, her determination to succeed had come from. Jessie hadn't said so, but it was clear she saw Ruth's father in the girl, the father who hadn't been around to see her grow up because of his determination to succeed.

They also hoped she'd settle down, get married, have a family — though goodness knows they had sense enough not to tell her that! She didn't, of course. Ruth Hannacker lived her life on her terms.

"Packing, gathering everything up ... I guess that made it all real."

Riley and Jessie aren't moving completely out of the old Hannacker place; they're just "swapping places" with Willa. When the fresh-out-of-agriculture-school twenty-one-year-old went to work with her grandfather on the family farm seven years ago, Riley'd put a small addition on the house so she'd have her own private apartment. Now that Willa will be running the whole farm, she'll move into the "big house," and the grandparents will have the little apartment to come home to when they visit. No, not visit. They'll spend the spring, summer, and fall at their lakeside cabin, but nobody wants to be on a lake in the wintertime — the water no longer bright blue but dull gray, reflecting off winter clouds.

Winter is Thanksgiving and Christmas. They'd be home in Callison County for all that.

"What is it about the 'real' that bothers you?"

"I don't ... want it to be over."

"Life?"

Another withering look.

"That's not what I mean, but I don't like any of the words for what I do mean. You know, like 'contributing,' or 'mattering' or 'making a difference.'" Jessie did hate what she called "designer words." "I just don't want to be ... done. Retired. Where the younger people keep on playing the game and I sit in the stands watching."

"You wouldn't make a very good cheerleader."

"Riley, I'm serious."

He can see she is then. Totally serious. He takes both her hands in his.

"We'll stay ... involved." It's the only word he can think to use.

"Promise me? Promise me that we'll be a part of what's happening. And with the family — we need to be there ... not just for the kids, but with them. Promise me we'll always have some skin in the game."

RILEY HAD PROMISED, of course. Swore they'd always play a part in their children's lives. It had mattered to Jessie way more than it had to him, but Riley Hannacker would have given his precious Jessie anything. Anything at all. Now she was gone.

Back and forth.

Back and forth.

He listened, tried to hear the chair make a sound. But it was silent.

Chapter Six

It was more than an hour before Willa's battered pickup truck pulled in beside Ruth's rented Honda next to the rock lying on the roadside of McCubbin Lane. Ruth was waiting for her there when she pulled in.

Usually it was Willa who did the babbling, talking nonstop, words with the force of a blast from a fire hose, about anything and everything and nothing in between. Today it was Ruth who babbled, and not because part of Willa's jaw was still numb. Ruth hadn't told her cousin what she'd found and why she wanted Willa to drop what she was doing and come running. Partly because Ruth wanted to see the look on Willa's face when the whole mystery was revealed. But also because Ruth felt uneasy about pouring out the whole story on a cell phone.

She had come back down to her car to wait for Willa, needed to show her the way up, of course, but it was equally important that she not remain in the cave, not go back in there until Willa was with her.

After all, the Tree House was not hers. The money there had been Willie Ray's portion of the Cornbread

Mafia spoils, the only thing the feds didn't confiscate when they busted the organization. Obviously, her father and mother believed the Tree House had been handed down to the remaining members of the Cornbread Mafia when Willie Ray died. Her mother had used an untold amount of it to help out the families of the men who'd been busted in weed fields all over the country. And now, the Tree House belonged to … who? Why, it belonged to *Dad*, of course. And he hadn't given anybody permission to go there, might not even be happy to know she knew the Tree House existed. Ruth didn't want the whole responsibility for this breach of her father's private affairs credited to her own private account. She wanted to share the discovery … spread the *guilt* around with her father's precious grand-child. If Dad didn't take it well, he certainly wouldn't explode all over Willa!

And besides, Ruth wasn't even certain what the next step in the progression ought to be. It'd seemed obvious in the beginning that she had to talk to her father about the find. But did she? Should she? Yeah, her mother had "given" the Tree House to Ruth … but it really belonged to Dad. It did, didn't it? Did that mean she had some kind of obligation to let him know she knew it existed, that she'd seen it? Should she just … let sleeping dogs lie, forget about the whole thing? But how could she do a thing like that now?

Ruth gushed fire-hose style at Willa the moment she pulled to a stop in her truck. She should have simply handed her mother's letter to Willa and that would have explained everything, but she hadn't brought it with her, so she just babbled out the tale in her own words. Some part of her stood outside herself as she told the tale to Willa, marveling at how at this moment the two of them had switched personas. Willa had been shocked into temporary silence, and Ruth was chattering away like a magpie.

Willa's eyes grew bigger and bigger with every word.

Ruth understood that she needed to get a better grip on herself, but she'd allowed the tight rein she kept on her emotions to loosen because she needed it. She needed the release of such un-paralleled, unexpected joy. It was a warm breath on the cold fingers of her grief.

"You mean there's——?"

"A fortune buried in a cave up there? Yup."

"How much money?"

"I don't know. I didn't take the time to count it."

"Is that what you wanted the legal pad for, to make some kind of tally sheet?"

"Yeah, but maybe I'm having second thoughts." She ran her fingers through her yellow-blonde hair. "I don't know anymore. I don't know if we ought to count it, if it's any of our business how much is there, if we ought to——"

"Well, I *do* know that I want to see it. We'll figure out what comes next after that."

It took a whole lot less time to climb up to the Tree House from the road this time than it had taken at first, but Ruth was aware that they should be careful not to leave a trail, a path somebody could follow. There was, after all, a bank vault with who knew how much money — thousands of dollars, surely — in it sitting here unguarded. She was sure her mother and the others had taken similar precautions and it made her feel a kinship with all of them that she found strangely comforting.

Ruth was finally rewarded with what she'd been looking forward to — the look of slack-jawed amazement on Willa's face when Ruth showed her cousin the cave entrance, the vault door and the interior of the tanker beyond. She should have pulled out her cell phone and taken a picture!

"I … I can't leave without knowing how much money is here," Ruth said. "I don't think that's inappropriate — do you? I mean, maybe we talk about this to Dad or maybe we don't, but I'd like a better idea of what all this — is worth — before we start any kind of discussion."

"It is, after all, 'ill-gotten gains,'" Willa pointed out, "subject to forfeiture—"

"If anybody could prove where it came from — which they couldn't. And if somebody got their hands on it — which they won't."

In the light of the lantern Willa had brought, Ruth set about designing a meticulous balance sheet — a record of how much money was in each box. Even in the lantern light, it was hard to count the bills, so Ruth carefully took each one of the cash boxes out to the opening of the cave between the rocks where she could see the contents in the sunlight. She became absorbed in the task — tossing comments out to Willa, who had started at the other end of the shelf making her own ledger.

"I wonder why some of these are crisp, new thousand-dollar bills and others are old used twenties?"

"Your mother must have done some currency switches over the years — to keep people from noticing the expenditures, do you think?"

Ruth thought about that and postulated a couple of theories of her own, then bent to the task at hand, making sure she counted accurately — each box twice — recorded the numbers accurately, and got an error-free total.

At some point, Ruth noticed that Willa had stopped counting the bills in the cash boxes. The girl had dropped to the floor and was sitting Indian fashion, with the quart jars of whatever-it-was beside her, poring over the ledger books that had been on the shelf with them.

Ruth lost track of time, but when she finished the final tabulation of the last box, she was sure it'd been hours since they started counting. Willa was lost in the ledger book on her lap and barely looked up when Ruth made her grand pronouncement.

"Drum roll, please," Ruth said. "If my calculations are correct — and they are, I checked each one two times — the grand total of cash is a whopping seventy-six thousand, five hundred ninety dollars.

She expected to see Willa leap to her feet and do her happy dance, which Papa'd once described as "a walrus giving birth to farm equipment." She didn't, though, didn't even get up, just lifted her eyes from the book in her lap with a look on her face Ruth couldn't read.

"What's up with you? Why aren't you bouncing off the walls? Aren't you excited? This thing," Ruth made a gesture that encompassed the whole tanker, "is worth more than seventy-six thousand dollars."

"Actually, no it's not."

"You think I didn't count it right?"

"No, you just didn't count it *all.*"

"Yes I did, I numbered each of the cash boxes and listed a total of the money in each one."

"You counted all the cash, but you didn't count *everything.*"

Ruth had no idea what Willa was talking about.

"I was just about to run a few numbers of my own." Willa held up her cellphone showing the calculator app. "But I don't need a calculator to figure out that all *this,*" she gestured toward the jars that'd been on the shelf where she'd found the ledger book, "is worth ..." She paused.

"*Millions.* Maybe tens of millions — depends on the market."

"Market for what?"

She pointed to the jars. "Do you know what's in these jars?"

"Pinto beans?" Ruth guessed.

Willa laughed, her musical contagious laugh, but Ruth was too thoroughly confused to join in.

"Not beans, seed. *Marijuana* seed."

All the air went out of Ruth's belly.

"Seriously?" She had never actually seen a marijuana seed.

"Not just *any* marijuana seed. These are *Righteous Weed seeds.*" She tapped the ledger books in her lap. "Willie Ray documented everything, every location, every strain, everything. These are the seeds the Cornbread Mafia used to grow the finest strain of marijuana ever developed. They called it Baby Bear's Bed, because it was 'just right.'"

"Are you telling me you could sell those jars of seed for millions of dollars? Is that why Willie Ray stored them here?"

"I doubt it. He probably wasn't even thinking about that. This is just the perfect place to store seed — cool, dark and dry. And I guess you *could* sell the seed. If you could find the right buyer. You wouldn't even want to try, though, until you had a patent, firm and secure in your hip pocket."

"A patent? On seeds?"

"No, you can't get a patent on seed. You'd have to grow some of it, patent the plant. And if you decided to *grow* it ..." She tilted her head back. "Whew, doggies! Do it right and—"

"What does marijuana sell for? Like, a pound of it?"

"The market has stabilized in the past couple of years,

not such huge swings. You could count on … minimum, five hundred dollars."

"Five hundred dollars for *one* pound?"

"For outdoor weed, yeah."

"And how many pounds of it could you get from say, an acre?"

"Two thousand, give or take."

Ruth didn't need a calculator to run those numbers.

"That's a million dollars!"

"For *outdoor* cannabis … *legal* cannabis." Willa cocked her head to the side. "There's more than one way to skin a cat."

Ruth just stared at Willa, probably gaped at her.

"How do you know all this?"

Willa laughed again, that musical sound.

"My last name's Hannacker and I'm from Callison County! Show up at the University of Kentucky School of Agriculture with that combination and weed's the subject of every conversation. And suddenly everybody wants to be your new best friend."

Ruth had a startling thought.

"Wait a minute. That seed's what …? Thirty, no forty, maybe forty-*five* years old. Will it still grow?"

"Not but one way to find out." Willa grinned. "Plant it and see."

Chapter Seven

Willa sat in her truck for a few moments beside the big rock after Ruth pulled out and drove away. Her fingers hovered over her cell phone, eager to call Isaiah and gush out the story. But he always turned his phone off when he went into a meeting and he wouldn't likely turn it back on again until late this afternoon. She was soooo tempted to leave him some kind of enigmatic voicemail — but no, that was childish. Fun, yes, but childish. Willa had to *talk* to him, couldn't wait to share the exciting news!

Or not.

Might be Isaiah wouldn't think it was exciting. *That* was a sobering thought. In fact, Willa had no idea what Isaiah would think about buried weed money. Maybe she shouldn't even mention it. Riiiight, just blow by the most thrilling thing that'd happened to her since ... she couldn't even remember anything comparable. Why would she want to keep a thing like that from Isaiah?

Oh, boy, here we go again — the image of the seesaw in her elementary school playground, the one she'd fallen off umpteen gazillion times, flashed yet again into her mind. It was the perfect metaphor for her relationship with Isaiah.

She loved him. She genuinely did. Willa knew that much for lead pipe certain. But nothing else about their relationship was simple or easy or as for-sure as her love.

Isaiah Montgomery had sat down in the seat next to hers on a flight from Phoenix to Dallas-Fort Worth International Airport last summer, after he gave up his first-class seat to a mother with a squalling baby.

"That was nice of you," she'd said.

"Naaa, not really. Airplanes are like school busses — all the cool kids sit in the back."

She was returning to Kentucky from a rock-climbing trip in Yosemite; he was returning to Atlanta from a raft trip on the Colorado River through the Grand Canyon. He said he was a corporate attorney; she said she was a farmer. He said his secret vice was eating peanut butter out of the jar with a spoon at three o'clock in the morning; she said she carried a salt shaker in her shirt pocket so she could pick tomatoes off the vine and eat them while they were still warm. He said his favorite movie was *The Matrix*, he loved classical music, particularly Rachmaninov's Piano Concerto No 2 and he was a liberal Democrat. She said her favorite movie was *Toy Story*, her favorite song was "Pretty Woman" by Roy Orbison and she was a conservative Republican. They both missed their connecting flights so they could go to dinner somewhere besides the airport — and take their masks off.

"Actually, I don't even care if you're homely under that mask," he'd said. "The red hair covers a multitude of sins."

"Well, I do care if you're homely. Black hair, black skin, brown eyes — too monochromatic. You need to cultivate some flashier attributes."

They spent the night together, and had carved out time to be with each other at every possible opportunity for the past six months — bickering and teasing and arguing and making love. He'd begun pointing out that the current state of working remotely meant he could live just about anywhere he wanted. She'd begun envisioning a yard full of dark-skinned, dark-eyed children with red hair and freckles.

But she had absolutely no idea how Isaiah would respond to the Tree House and the Pandora's Box of possibilities it opened up. She'd told him her family history, but still …

One thing Willa *did* know for certain was that she and Ruth should have cancelled the family supper scheduled for that night, come up with some kind of excuse — Willa had burned the beans or something. Anybody'd believe that. She tried to talk Ruth into putting it off, but her cousin stuck her nose into her laptop the moment they got back to the house and only came up for air long enough to ask Willa for pencils — "not pens, I need to be able to erase the figures" — and to say that after supper tonight the two of them had *a lot* to talk about.

But Ruth had blown off Willa's warning about the evening — how you couldn't spend a whole day contemplating a pirate's treasure of more than seventy-five thousand dollars, and a pirate's trove worth millions, and then sit down to dinner with your family and grieving grandfather without somebody figuring out something was up.

To make matters worse, Willa's younger sister Lissa called and said her family couldn't come — Joel was out of town and Lissa had a migraine. She'd suffered from such headaches all her life, but it was always worse when she was pregnant. Their fifth child was due this fall. If there was one thing Lissa's four children — ages six, five, three and eighteen months — could be counted on to do, it was provide distraction. Especially the youngest, McKenna. Grampa called her Kenny Girl. The child had recently discovered how to scream in a high-pitched voice that threatened to crack crystal. Willa thought it sounded like a dying pterodactyl. Adult conversation was difficult with the whole crew around, and that would have been a blessing.

Then Mom called about five o'clock to say she'd decided to "hang out with the grands tonight" — translate that: "I'm going to try to keep the noise level somewhere below the 170 decibels of a jet engine during takeoff, so Lissa's head doesn't explode." Now, instead of a family dinner with seven adults and four screaming children, there'd be only Dad, Grandpa, herself and Ruth. Willa's father, Drew, was an uncannily sensitive and intuitive man, attuned to nuances in the feelings of the people around him. Without his grandchildren crawling all over him, he'd pick up on some vibe, she was sure of it.

But as it turned out, Willa was wrong about that part. It hadn't been her father who outed them. Oh, he'd started sniffing around the edges of it early on, but in the end she and her cousin hadn't needed anybody's help to blow the whole thing.

Chapter Eight

Drew Hannacker looked at his watch and then went to the kitchen window. He needed to get his mother inside and "settled" with the housekeeper before he left for supper at Dad's with Ruth and Willa. Andrea was already gone, had left half an hour ago to help with the kids while Lissa lay in a darkened room upstairs, her head in the pounding vice grip of a migraine.

"Gotcha!" came a cry from the garden beside the back porch, and he looked up to see his mother, floppy hat pulled low over her forehead, a look of studied concentration and determination on her sweating face, hacking at the dirt with a hoe.

And he thought about what that first doctor had said to them all those years ago when Mom first started behaving bizarrely — back before it got so bad she had to move in with him and Andrea.

"When you've seen one case of dementia," the doctor had said, "you've seen ... *one case of dementia*."

Meaning, as they would soon learn, that every case of dementia was an individual event, as different from every other case as the fingerprints of those whose brains were being riddled like swiss cheese by everything from Alzheimer's, to frontotemporal and vascular dementia. Doctors explained that dementia wasn't a specific disease, but rather a group of conditions characterized by a loss of thinking ability, memory, attention, logical reasoning, and other mental abilities so severe that it interferes with daily functioning. None of the handful of brain disorders had a conclusive diagnosis, could only be confirmed "after the fact" through an autopsy. The only way to diagnose a living patient was by the process of elimination — one by one, you eliminated all the other things the symptoms couldn't be. And more often than not, you didn't end up with a single disorder, a last man standing, but a handful of the most likely candidates.

Sherry Lynn stopped working for long enough to wipe the sweat off her brow, then bent back to ruthlessly chopping down and removing every tomato plant seedling in the garden. Oh, she didn't believe they were tomato plants. She was certain they were weeds and there was no convincing her otherwise, and she went after them with a relentless hatred.

"You think you're gonna take over my garden, do you," she growled under her breath. "Well, you got another three or four more thinks coming!"

Drew's mother currently exhibited the symptoms of three, no, four different mental conditions. Her Alzheimer's symptoms included memory problems — forgetting events and people — and asking the same question over and over. Those were coupled with the vascular dementia symptoms of depression and inappropriate emotional responses. Frontotemporal dementia had been the frontrunner in the beginning because most cases were diagnosed in people aged forty-five to sixty-five and his mother had been sixty-one when she decided one day out of the blue to chase down every chicken in the chicken house in the back yard, more than a dozen of them. She had systematically wrung their necks, one after another, stuffed the chicken carcasses into a garbage bag and walked around her neighborhood in Brewster, depositing a dead chicken on the porch of every house she passed. That was also when she began to experience personality changes and a "lack of social awareness."

"You need to get yourself a jockstrap, Father," she told young Father MacWhorter one Sunday after church. "That lump in your robe looks like you got an erection."

The obsessive behavior — determined to, say, rescue the whole tomato garden from an infestation of weeds — had only recently appeared, along with more troubling symptoms that didn't fit neatly into any of the baskets. Sometimes Drew wondered if his mother'd had a stroke or suffered from a brain tumor.

Hallucinations were among the newer charms on her dementia bracelet.

She saw buzzards lined up like blackbirds on the clothesline, a shark in the creek that ran by the house, had climbed up on a kitchen chair screaming in terror the other day at the lobster with fangs crawling on the floor. Lately, though, she seemed to spend most of her time in the past — talked about things that'd happened decades ago as if she were experiencing them in real time. Two weeks ago, she hid in her room all day from the FBI agent who had shown up at Drew's ninth birthday party and arrested her. Her most consistent emotion was an overwhelming sadness, expressed in sobbing for hours, over losing "all my beautiful things" — the contents of the tacky mansion they'd lived in forty years ago.

Sherry Lynn suddenly stopped chopping, stood up

straight and pushed her short white hair back off her sweaty forehead.

"Oh, Steve, you say the sweetest things."

Drew cringed. She'd recently resurrected the man who drugged her four decades ago to get the information that should have landed her alongside his father in federal prison.

She giggled at the not-there hunk today. But her typical emotional response to those ghosts of Christmas past was almost always an off-the-charts rage — a fury unlike any he'd seen since those awful months after Jessie told her that Drew's father Riley was Ruth's father, too.

He dreaded the day, which he feared might not be long in coming, when he'd have to put his mother into some kind of custodial care facility that was equipped to deal with outbursts of violence. Oh, she might wake up in the morning as docile as a kitten, but a homicidal rage was only a heartbeat or two away. Andrea and the part-time housekeeper/caregiver Wanda Pruitt could only barely control his mother now, when all she did to vent her rage was curse, wail and throw things. If that escalated to real violence …

Though small and petite, his mother suffered from no physical maladies to accompany her mental decline. The woman was remarkably strong and healthy. She had started taking Jazzercise in the 1980s and later became an instructor, conducted classes three times a week in the basement of the Methodist church for more than a decade. She could probably outrun both of them — with Andrea's arthritic knees and the constricted movement in Drew's left leg occasioned by a femur fracture when a horse fell on him. Other than the medications to ameliorate the symptoms of her various mental conditions, Sherry Lynn didn't take a single other prescription drug.

No high blood pressure. No high cholesterol. No sign of heart disease or coronary artery disease. She'd actually taken up running for awhile in her mid-fifties when one of the roll-call of step-children from her five marriages was training for a marathon. She gave up running — stopped abruptly — when the mental issues began … it actually seemed like from one day to the next she forgot she was a runner. She still loved to take long walks — like four- or five-mile-long walks — and that would soon become an issue again with summer coming on. He didn't like her wandering all over the farm for fear she would get lost.

His cell phone rang and he pulled it from his pocket, saw Willa's name on the screen.

"Hey sweetheart," he said.

"You gonna be much longer? Ruth made cornbread and it actually looks edible — it'll be out of the oven in half an hour."

"I just have to get your grandmother corralled before I leave."

"Is she still chopping up the tomato plants?"

He looked out the window and saw that she'd stopped work to talk to someone who wasn't there.

"She's just about done, actually, just leaning on her hoe, chatting with … it's either the Easter Bunny, Donald Trump or the Boston Strangler."

"Donald Trump *or* the Boston Strangler … sounds like distinction without a difference to me."

"I see what you did there, thought you'd slip one in on me."

No Talking Politics was a sacred family rule — no exceptions! And so, of course, Willa was obliged to take every opportunity to needle the others with comments. He wondered if she did the same with Isaiah, the attorney who had only in the past couple of months begun to realize what his side had gotten the country into.

"Half an hour, Dad, or your cornbread will be cold."

He put his phone back into his pocket and went outside to see if he could herd his mother into the house.

"I. Hate. Weed," she grumbled, each word slathered in loathing.

Weed. Singular. Not weed*s*. Maybe she wasn't talking about the tomato sprouts before her. Weed — pot, cannabis, marijuana — had, after all, given his mother everything she'd ever wanted in life, and then snatched it all back out of her grasp again.

Chapter Nine

The family supper Ruth and Willa presided over was quiet and subdued. Ruth's cornbread was more than passable — nothing like Mom's, of course, but nobody could make cornbread like Willa's mother, or any other dish, for that matter. Mom was a fabulous cook. She could see a tribe of Taggart relatives pulling up in the driveway and have an impromptu supper on the table for the whole dozen of them in half an hour. Without ever getting a hair out of place or a speck of flour on the floor. Willa realized that the ability to cook wasn't an inheritable trait, but you'd think that after spending twenty-plus years in the presence of that kind of awesome-ness, some of it would have rubbed off on her. Not. Willa's sister Lissa, two years younger than her, had neither inherited nor absorbed it. Lissa had *cultivated* it — cooking, baking, sewing, cross-stitch — those were pursuits where she could excel and you could see how hard she concentrated to learn each new skill. Lissa hadn't breathed right away after birth, and the doctors thought that maybe her brain had been deprived of oxygen and that's why she was ... slow. A sweet, compliant child, Lissa struggled mightily in school, barely squeaked through, and suffered from debilitating migraine headaches that kept her home in bed for days at a time. She blossomed as a teenager, though, startlingly beautiful with long curly blonde hair and dimples, but it was her gentle, soft-spoken nature that had won the heart of the school's quarterback heartthrob Joel Castleton. When she married Joel, Lissa came into her own. They started a family right away and she was the consummate home-maker, loved everything about being a wife and mother, and was well on her way to fulfilling her Catholic obliga-tion to produce a houseful of children.

Conversation at supper was forced ... like all four of them had other things on their minds than interacting with each other. And at least three of them did. Clearly, Grandpa was thinking about Grandma. He was only pretending to eat the pinto beans Ruth had ladled out for him, moving them around in the bowl, stirring it as if hoping something would come up from the depths of it that would render it inedible and relieve him of the obliga-tion of eating it.

And she and Ruth were contemplating a buried trea-sure worth millions. Ruth surely was, because Dad had to ask the question twice before she answered him.

"Hello, knock, knock, Earth to Ruth — how long are you planning to stay?" he asked.

"I'm not sure. There's a lot more to do here than I thought there'd be." She shot a look at Willa. "You know, going through Mama's things."

"I didn't think Jessie had left much here when you guys moved to Tucker's Crossing. I helped carry those boxes!"

"She didn't, actually. Just some things in the attic. Personal items."

"Your mother had things in the attic?" Papa asked.

"Yeah, well, there wasn't much, and it was really old stuff."

"I didn't know there was *anything* of hers up there. How did you know?"

"I didn't. I need a new carry-on bag and I remembered there was luggage in the attic. When I went to look at it, I noticed some stuff behind the box of Christmas decorations and the Nativity scene. So whatever what had been there since before the last time we put up the big tree here."

After Willa's grandparents moved to their lake house, the Christmas celebration was officially handed down to the next generation. Willa's parents, Drew and Andrea, put on a mega-family gathering for all Hannackers and Taggarts, great and small, in the big Land's End mansion — which they rented out for the occasion like other large families did. Though her father owned the horse farm, Willa's parents didn't live in the "big house," too many bad memories for her father. Instead, he and Andrea had restored and renovated the historic old carriage house on the north side of the sprawling acreage beyond the horse barns and they donated the mansion to the Callison County Historical Society. The ladies in the society, with the help of the Chamber of Commerce, had tried to turn it into the same kind of attraction as My Old Kentucky Home in Bardstown that attracted thousands of visitors every year. But they were never able to pull it off. My Old Kentucky Home had the outdoor musical that celebrated the music of Stephen Foster, a nineteenth century songwriter who might or might not ever have set foot on the property. A hard act to follow when all you have at Land's End is a fountain shaped like a dolphin in the foyer — where her father and his father had come very close to dying. Nobody but family knew that story, though.

The family Christmas bash at Land's End only included her grand*father's* side of the family, of course, not her grand*mother's*. Her Grandma Sherry Lynn had been married multiple times, meaning Christmas celebrations with whatever happened to be their "new family" moved around a lot. But her parents faithfully attended, wherever the celebration was held. Drew Hannacker had taken the 'honor thy father *and thy mother* commandment' to heart when he was a kid, and even though he didn't fit in with the vibe of some of the other families *at all*, he always suited up and showed up like a good little soldier whenever it was required of him. And dragged her, Mom and Lissa along with him.

"Jessie never mentioned to me that she'd stored anything in the attic," Papa said.

Ruth fired a bail-me-out look at Willa, begging with her eyes for Willa to take a hand-off of the conversational ball.

Willa grabbed it — and promptly sank a three-point shot *in the wrong goal.*

"Maybe Grandma forgot she put it there."

"Forgot? What was in the boxes?"

"Oh, nothing special," Ruth said airily. "Some picture albums, the ones that used to be on the top shelf in the hall closet."

"The ones with pictures of you building snowmen in that field?" Willa offered, ready to launch the conversation toward the five best ways to construct a snowman, coal versus Oreos for eyes and maybe a soliloquy about why she hated the *Frosty the Snowman* Christmas special — the hero *melts* at the end, for crying out loud.

"Is that all? Just picture albums?"

"No. Other stuff, too. Some scarves and gloves, an old jewelry box and a—"

"Jewelry box? I never saw that. What was in it — certainly not jewelry. Jessie never wore anything but her wedding band."

Ruth looked decidedly uncomfortable.

"Well, you can use a jewelry box for other things, you know — it has drawers where you can put … cards and notes and … letters, stuff like that."

Willa could tell that her father had picked up on Ruth's discomfort. Despite their age difference, Drew and Ruth had been close as children, she had followed Drew around like a puppy. He'd spent as much time as he could manage at the farm because that's where Coco, the foal his father had given him for his ninth birthday, lived.

Raising Coco … that's when her father and the rest of the world discovered that Drew Hannacker was a true horse whisperer.

"So, Dad, you think Hazard Pay is going to be ready for the Derby?"

Willa sailed the non sequitur out into the air like a paper airplane. It dropped nose first into the bowl of beans in the center of the table.

"Cards and notes? Letters? Not from *me*."

Ruth had told her that when her father got out of prison he made a big deal out of putting all his letters to Jessie in a pile in the back yard and burning them.

Grandpa put his napkin down on the table and started to rise. "Where are they? I'd like to see them."

The stricken look on Ruth's face was unmistakable.

"They weren't *from* anybody, Dad. They were *to* …"

"*To* …?"

Everyone was aware that something was going on now. All eyes went to Ruth.

Ruth looked at Willa. The others at the table followed

the look like a volley in a tennis match. Grandpa's gaze went from one to the other.

"Am I missing something here?"

Ruth's look asked Willa if she should continue to bob and weave. Willa's look ran up the white flag. Game over.

Chapter Ten

Riley almost lost it when he saw Jessie's handwriting, words she'd put down on that sheet of paper for her daughter. It was almost like stumbling upon a new photo of her. He had looked at all the pictures of Jessie. Many of them had been at the lake house, and Riley'd feared they were lost forever. But Ruth assured him they'd been saved in iCloud and though he had only a vague idea what that meant, he was grateful when she downloaded the images for him. He'd stared into Jessie's face, her eyes, studied her, memorized her. And after awhile, his memories of her conjured up the pictured images. Almost like he couldn't see her real face, just the image of it that'd been captured in a camera in a frozen moment in time.

Then, he'd happen upon a new photo. One he didn't remember, hadn't yet memorized. And for just a moment the newness brought her essence back to him. Didn't last long, but the warmth somehow melted the ice encasing his heart, just for a little while anyway.

Now he sat staring in the dancing flames of the fire

while Drew read the letter Ruth had gone up to her room to retrieve for him. It had begun "My precious Ruthie ..."

It was written after Jessie'd been in that wreck. God, that'd been a nightmare, sitting in a prison cell, knowing she was hurt but not knowing how bad, knowing she was in pain but he couldn't be there to comfort her. Knowing she was scared and he wasn't there to chase the Boogie Man back into the closet.

The wreck had been a wake-up call, he supposed, had made her realize that she might not always be around to take care of Ruth. If something happened to her before Riley got out of prison ... Jessie'd wanted to be able to reach back up out of the grave and help her daughter if Ruth needed it.

So she'd told Ruth about Willie Ray's Tree House.

Riley remembered the conversation they'd had about it, how he and Jessie didn't realize Willie Ray was serious at first, and then they'd tried — to no avail — to talk him out of it.

"FINE," Riley says. "Your tanker idea makes sense. Just got one question."

He pauses and Riley's got him now.

"Just explain to me how you plan to jam that tanker through the three-foot opening of that cave."

"Ain't gonna take it in through the front door," Willie Ray says with a grin. "I'm gonna dig a hole in that meadow, bust through the top of the cave, lower the tanker down, then fill in the hole with dirt around it — just leave a little space in front so's you can get into the cave and open the tanker door."

. . .

HE AND JESSIE had talked about the Tree House while he was in prison, using their own special code. Jessie had told him how she had needed the resources there and what she'd done with them. Without actually spelling it out, she'd let him know that she was gradually changing the cash there out for other cash, because old bills were systematically taken out of circulation.

She told him about using the money there to buy a double-wide trailer house for the Haskins when their home burned to the ground while Ralph was locked up in Kansas.

For Pete Plover's wife's heart surgery and a new pickup truck when Orville Richards's sixteen-year-old totaled his. Over the years, the Tree House had funded dozens, maybe even hundreds of needs in the community occasioned by the arrests of a hundred men who worked for the Cornbread Mafia.

But eventually that part was over. One by one, the men were released, went home to their families, created new lives. Jessie had invested the money, slowly and secretly, over the years, built up an impressive stock portfolio. By the time Riley was released, the two of them could have kicked back and not hit a lick at a snake for the rest of their lives. They didn't, of course. Life was about working and contributing, a hard days' labor, producing the kind of muscle and mind tired that fueled a sense of accomplishment.

The Tree House money had paid for Jessie to go to college at night and during the summer until she had an elementary school teaching certificate. It had purchased for Ruth the best education money could buy, as it had financed uncounted other college educations for the offspring of Cornbread Mafia men. Riley wondered sometimes if the per capita rate of college graduates in Callison County was higher than the state average on that account.

He glanced at Drew, bent over the letter, processing it. Well, in some ways, maybe this was best. Riley hadn't ever considered how he might tell his family about the Tree House someday. He and Jessie had talked about it a time or two, but that was when life was simple and predictable and you counted on the implicit assurance that when you went to bed at night you'd been issued an ironclad guarantee from the universe that you would wake up safe and sound there the next morning.

"Grandpa … are you mad at us?" Willa asked. As if it was even possible for him to harbor anger in his heart toward the little red-haired spitfire that brought joy and laughter into the lives of everyone she met.

"I guess I should have taken the letter to you as soon as I found it," Ruth said. But he wasn't the least bit surprised that she hadn't. Willa probably would have, if it'd been up to her. Not Ruth. Blame it on a difference in temperament, of course, but it was more than that.

He'd missed out on Ruth's growing-up years, missed out on that bonding that happens just naturally by daily association, by participating in the mundane occurrences in other people's everyday lives. He had done everything he could to make up for that loss, and he could see Ruth trying, too. But it was a gap too wide to bridge, and he'd given up making the effort a long time ago. They had a great relationship — he loved her desperately and she loved him right back. The two of them had stored up in their minds at every prison visit enough of the other to last them until they could get another helping. It'd been a starvation diet, though, and both of them had come out of those years apart emotionally malnourished — with the lasting effects as visible as the bent bones of scurvy in men on ships who didn't get enough vitamin C. "I just got so excited … like a little kid, wanted to go dig up the treasure, so I—"

"You don't have to explain. I get it." He turned to Willa. "And no, pumpkin, I am not mad at you." Back to Ruth. "Either one of you."

"I didn't know about this." Drew held out the letter in his hand. "The Tree House specifically, anyway. But I supposed now and then that there was … some source of income that was … above and beyond. The time Jessie paid the veterinarian bill after Coco was sick, I suspected there had to be some stash of cash around somewhere." He grinned. "Never would have thought it was anything as elaborate as—"

"As a tanker full of weed money buried out in a field somewhere in the county," Willa finished for him. "The great myth, real after all."

Riley turned to face them all, indicated the tally sheet that Ruth had given him about the money in the cash boxes. "I haven't been to the Tree House in … years, I guess. So I suppose it is a good thing your mother had the sound judgement to tell you about it. Otherwise," he paused and the agony of his loss sliced down all the way to his bone marrow, "I might not have come back either, you know, and then …"

He didn't want to go there, to be there in that place of pain and certainly didn't want to drag the others there with him. So he pushed through, went on.

"At any rate, the cat is officially out of the bag. What's in the Tree House … it belongs to all of us. Do any of you have any thoughts on what we do with what's in there? Seventy-six thousand dollars is a boatload of money." He actually found a smile. "We could stage the mother of all parties, buy booze for the whole county, spend a week in drunken debauchery — Willie Ray would grin his gums dry at that."

"There's more than just money in the Tree House, Dad." Ruth's gaze pierced him. And in that millisecond before the next words came, he felt the import of them, some great powerful force rushing at him out of the darkness, and he knew that when it struck, it would knock all the pilings out from under the life he had built in the past forty years.

"Seed," Willa said. "Righteous Weed seed. There's enough to grow fifty acres of it. A hundred acres … maybe more than that, depending on how much of it will actually germinate after all these years."

Drew spoke when Riley couldn't find words.

"Whoa, there. You're not suggesting—?"

"That we grow it?" Ruth said. "I think we at least have to consider the possibility, have the conversation. It's worth … *millions*."

Chapter Eleven

"I don't know how much any of you know about the state of cannabis in America in 2022," Ruth said. "I knew absolutely zero until six hours ago. I'm no expert now, but I've spent every minute since Willa and I climbed back down that hillside scouring the internet for information. I've made phone calls to some bankers I know, some money managers, even some … unsavory types who—"

"You know a criminal or two," Riley finished for her. "So do I."

Ruth flushed a little, but plunged ahead.

"For simplicity's sake, let's just pretend all of us are as ignorant as I was this morning. I'll give you a down and dirty of what I found out since then, an info dump, so we are all singing from the same sheet of music."

Riley supposed he was in some kind of shock, because it flat-out didn't seem real to him that he was sitting in the living room of the home where he'd grown up, talking to his children and grandchildren about getting back into the weed business that had taken from him *twenty years* of his life.

As Ruth continued to speak, he found himself more and more surprised by what she had been able of find out in just one afternoon's search of the internet. He had so far distanced himself from any and all things related to marijuana when he got out of prison that he knew nothing at all about it — was totally content with that. Now, sitting here snug in his old-geezer-can't-do-technology suit, he was staggered by the breadth and depth of information available on the subject with just a couple of strokes on a keyboard.

He supposed it might be true what he'd heard — that you could build a nuclear bomb from instructions online. Don't try this at home.

"… is the most important issue," Ruth was saying when he tuned back in. "Will it grow? After all this time, more than forty years, will the seed in Willie Ray's Tree House grow?" She shot a glance at Willa. "I asked my cousin, who has far more expertise in agribusiness than I do and she gave me an extremely complex, complicated, technical, involved and convoluted answer that went something like this. 'We'll have to grow it and see.'"

Willa did a little bow.

"Using cell culture techniques that seem as magical to me and sprinkling fairy dust," Ruth said, "it appears it's possible to make a synthetic embryo of ancient seeds."

"A lab in California did that from seeds found in an Egyptian tomb and a couple of months later, they had a stand of wheat," Willa put in. "I am not suggesting we'd have to go that far, but we absolutely would have to get a patent on the plant. Until we do, anybody could steal it and grow it. Happens more often than people realize. A couple of months ago, Monsanto discovered that the Chinese were stealing their premium corn technology. Corn was right out there in a field, and they took it."

"Here is what I found out that struck a chord with me," Ruth said. "It's how we could get the biggest bang for our buck — minimum effort, maximum payout. I read an article by the head of a big cannabis company titled 'The Holy Grail of Marijuana.' Apparently, weed growers are all looking for it."

"I knew that much," Willa says. She looked at her grandfather. "It's all about the myth, the legend, the mystique surrounding the first time a person got high. Twenty years ago, thirty. There's a universal nostalgia for the 'first time' sensation."

Riley remembered sitting in the frying-pan heat of Fire Base Eagle's Nest with soldiers who'd died in the mud there six months later — taking their first tokes off a "cigarette" Ace had rolled, using the grass clippings from a sandwich bag in his pocket.

"IF YOU GUYS IS FARMERS, *you must know about hemp. This here's a kissin' cousin to hemp.*"

"*My grandfather raised hundreds of acres during the war,*" *Riley says. "I'd heard you could smoke it and it'd feel a little like getting drunk.*"

"*You have to keep cows out of it,*" *says Ronnie Benson. "Screws up the milk.*"

"*But you saying didn't none of you ever* try *it?*" *Ace is incredulous.*

Riley looks at Willie Ray and winks.

"*We don't need nothing else to get high on — moonshine does the job just fine.*"

Ace feigns shock. "But ain't moonshine … illegal?"

"*Yup,*" *Riley says.*

"*So's weed.*"

Ace takes another drag off what he calls a "joint" and holds it out to Riley, who shakes his head.

"Don't smoke," he says.

"That don't matter. This ain't the same thing. You drink moonshine to get it into your blood. Well, you get the weed into your blood by smoking it."

Riley has taken an instant liking to the Harlem soldier but he has no desire to smoke the joint the man has rolled. He does, though. What the hell.

Taking a big lungful of the acrid smoke into his lungs, he immediately coughs it back out. Keeps coughing and coughing, his eyes watering. Ace chuckles the whole time.

"Feels like I just inhaled burning garbage."

"Like I said, the smoking part ain't the point. It's how you feel after that's the point."

The other guys gather around, pass the joint from one to another. Riley, Andy and Willie Ray. David Monaghan, Ben Higgs, Ronnie Benson, Kenny Taylor and Randy Nickel. None of them manages to draw it in with the ease Ace does, and then hold their breaths like he does. Well, except Tommy. Five Cents holds the joint out to his invisible friend and Tommy doesn't cough a single time.

When the joint is burned down to ash, Ace immediately rolls another one. He takes a drag off it, holds it out to Riley, who almost refuses, but doesn't. As the joint goes around and around the group of soldiers, Ace describes his "line of work."

"This here's what I do. Correction — did. Sell weed on the street in Harlem. It's how I made my living before Uncle Sam issued me the cordial invitation to give up my life of easy money, drugs, booze and beautiful women to join him in a fun-filled adventure here in scenic Vi-et-naaam. Now, I sell it here." He pauses then, looks from one to another of them. "How you boys feeling?"

Riley doesn't feel anything. But Willie Ray definitely does.

"I feel ... strange ... and ..."

"Mellow?" Ace suggests.

"Yeah," Willie says, and grins a stupid grin. "Yeah, mellow."

By suppertime, every one of the guardsmen is so high the world has become a glorious place. And they can't wait to get in the chow line because they're famished.

Riley feels as hungry as he did when he could smell the turkey cooking in Jean Taggart's kitchen, and she had shooed him and all her offspring out on pain of death and dismemberment if any of them dared to "get under foot again" while she finishes up Thanksgiving dinner.

"I was just thinking about my mama's Thanksgiving dinner," Willie Ray says, and Riley bursts out laughing. Everything seems funny.

"I was too!" he cries. "How good it smelled."

"And she wouldn't let anybody in the kitchen—" Andy says.

"Shooed us out with the broom—" Willie Ray says.

"So we sat in the dining room waiting," Riley says.

"We didn't just wait, we stole biscuits," says Andy.

"Yeah, biscuits," Willie Ray says.

Suddenly, the thought of Willie Ray's mother's homemade biscuits slathered in home-churned butter sounds so good Riley's mouth actually waters.

Ace looks around at the group and nods.

"It's called 'the munchies.'"

"Huh?" Andy asks.

"That sensation you gentlemen is feeling right now. Good weed makes you powerful hungry."

Riley and the others almost trample each other to get to the mess hall.

"Are you in line or ain't you?" Willie Ray asks Riley. "'Cause if you don't get out of my way, I'm going to start chewing on your leg."

Weed. Marijuana. The same plant Papa'd grown because the government had paid him to, acres and acres of it.

"If I'd known you could smoke that stuff growing along the fence rows, I coulda saved a fortune on cigarettes," Willie Ray says.

"It wouldn't have made you feel like this, though," Ace says. *"This here weed … it's* righteous."

"FOUR DECADES AGO, Righteous Weed was providing a first-time high to who knows how many weed smokers all over America," Ruth said. "It was the best weed on the market."

"Baby Bear's Bed," Drew spoke for the first time. "That's what Uncle Willie Ray called it because it was 'just right.'"

"And *that's* the selling point," Ruth said, her eyes shining. In that moment, she looked so much like her mother it made Riley's chest ache. "We would be all about quality, not quantity. Not hundreds of acres of it on farms all over the country. We'd grow what they call "boutique cannabis" — and that stuff sells for ten times what you can get for outside weed."

"If you've got the magic — and Righteous Weed is magic — you can get absolutely top dollar," Willa said. "Four thousand, maybe forty-five hundred dollars a pound."

"Seriously?" Drew said, awed.

Willa made a cross on the front of her shirt over her heart. "If I'm lying, I'm dying. As a matter of fact, outside-grown weed is now considered second- or third-rate stuff."

Riley marveled at how much everything had changed.

Willa described what she knew about the process by which outside cannabis was commercially grown and harvested, said it was, "kinda like shucking corn."

"Harvesting the industrial way with machinery, you could process forty acres of weed, called a 'biomass,' and concentrate it into hash in two weeks — using the extraction method to remove all the THC, PCB and terpenes."

Riley thought about how Willie Ray and Wazzi, the college professor/botanist, had communicated in what the others called "weed speak." Clearly, the fundamental "plant sex" that had so fascinated Willie Ray had since progressed to the level of test-tube babies and artificial insemination.

"We'd call it handcrafted, hand-harvested, hand-trimmed, select grown … things like that," Ruth said. "People are looking for something more than some big corporate Budweiser operation like Green Thumb Industries in Chicago, Aphria and Organigram in Canada, Cronos Group, or Tilray."

"The mystique of the very weed they smoked when they were kids …" Willa grinned. "Yeah, people would pay big bucks for that."

As he watched Willa's animated face, Riley thought — *she's us. We were about her age when we were riding high, didn't know we were circling the drain until it sucked us down. Were we really that young? That naive?*

"Right now, growing marijuana is legal in eleven states," Ruth said. "But the laws vary from state to state. In some states, it's legal to grow it but not sell it. In others, you can sell it but you have to bring it in from somewhere else. Every state that has legalized it requires that you have a license to grow it and all manner of regulations about how much you can grow. That's all over the map, too. Georgia issued six licenses this year. Oklahoma issued thousands — only for medicinal cannabis, of course, and only for sale to licensed dispensaries." She laughed. "The population of Oklahoma is maybe three million people and last year state-approved dispensaries filled four hundred thousand prescriptions for medicinal cannabis."

She paused and grew serious again.

"Strict licensing is to cut out folks like us," she said.

"The little guy. And that's how come *illegal* cannabis is still a far bigger enterprise in this country than legal weed. Big Canna has a powerful lobby, catering to industrial farmers. A license in some states will cost two million dollars, and you'd have to pay another two for license preparation."

Big Canna. Riley'd heard of Big Pharma, or Big Tech, didn't know there was a Big Canna, too.

Riley spoke for the first time. "If I'm hearing you right, sounds like you're suggesting the Hannacker family get back in the weed business. I been on that ledge where all of you is standin' right now. They's rocks at the bottom of that cliff that'll tear you apart. Lookin' down from the top, you think you can avoid 'em. But once you jump … you ain't got near as much say as you think over where you land."

Ruth tilted her head back and blew a tuft of air upward, floating the hair on her brow up in a puff. Jessie had written to Riley when Ruth learned to do the trick, saw that it entertained people and went around performing like an elephant standing on a ball everywhere she went. That'd been forty years ago.

"I'm not proposing anything. I'm just acknowledging that there are all kinds of options to consider."

She started ticking them off.

"Do we grow it at all? If so, where? Here? We don't have a license to grow it *anywhere* and getting one'd take months, maybe years … and there isn't enough money in the Tree House or in all our bank accounts put together to get one in a strict state. Grow it inside or outside? Say we could get a license for next year or 2024 in Oklahoma, grow it outside … just like Monsanto grew their premium strain of corn outside, and the Chinese stole it. What we've got, the special sauce that nobody else has is the reputation of Righteous Weed. That won't be worth Jack unless we're the only ones who have it."

"At the risk of being Captain Obvious here, last I checked it's still against the law to grow weed *in Kentucky*," Riley said.

She'd been pacing as she spoke and she stopped, looked from one to the other.

"I think we'd all agree that it won't be long — three years, five — before using/growing/selling cannabis in some form *will* be legal in Kentucky, legal everywhere in the whole country. It's the direction the culture's going. It's only a matter of time. We have a chance to get in early, establish ourselves. I'm not talking about forming some mammoth criminal organization here. This is a *legitimate business opportunity.*"

No, Riley thought, it's the Tar Baby.

"WHEN DID it get away from us?" Riley asks Willie Ray, who has been on the run for three days, barely one step ahead of the FBI. Growing weed had seemed innocent in the beginning, harmless. They didn't see the change. When had it darkened?

"Big money breeds evil same way a fly breeds maggots," Willie Ray says, his usually mobile face set, his eyes so very sad. "It's the Tar Baby. Don't look dangerous or bad, but soon's you touch it, you get stuck and ain't no way to let go."

Chapter Twelve

Willa watched the family's faces as Ruth gave what Willa thought of as the State of the Weed Address. Nope, this hadn't been the ideal way to unload the idea on everybody. Ruth was definitely shoving a boulder uphill. Willa wasn't anything like as tuned in and intuitive as her father, Drew, but she could read body language as well as most people and it was clear from the git-go that Ruth was playing to a tough crowd. Folded arms, guarded expressions — no outright hostility, which Willa took as a hopeful sign — but nothing open and receptive in the group's response, either.

And Willa? What did she think?

Why, she thought the idea of her family making a fortune growing a crop of Righteous Weed — whether legal or illegal — was a terrific idea.

No, it was complete insanity.

Yeah, *let's do it!* …

Hell no, this is crazy!

The moment she'd realized what was sealed in those jars in the Tree House, she had climbed aboard a roller-coaster and was hanging on with white-knuckled terror as it careened around obstacles and through a maze of possibilities.

Would they, could they, *should* they … *resurrect* the Cornbread Mafia?

Maybe.

Why not?

She and her cousins were the next generation, after all. And the thought of flipping the bird at the legal establishment that had stolen so very, very much from her family — that was *enormously* appealing. Of course, nobody'd ever dreamed there was any torch to pass, one to another. If Papa ever thought about the significance of the Righteous Weed seeds he knew were stored in the Tree House, he had certainly never shared those thoughts with her.

They had worked together hand-in-glove when she first got out of college — her gently nudging him toward the computerized methods of agribusiness she'd studied, him imparting a lifetime of farmer's wisdom you couldn't find in any textbook. They'd been close. She saw that he looked at her sometimes with a faraway expression on his face and she was sure he was remembering the best friend who had died at his feet, using his last breaths to tell a lie, saying he'd killed Jackson McClusky when it had really been Jessie who'd shot the man.

Jessie had told Ruth what happened that day in Big-un McClusky's hunting cabin and Ruth had told Willa.

Willa liked to think that in some small way, her presence in the world had given her grandfather back his best friend.

The growing understanding of the import of those jars of seed that'd been stored underground before the Reagan Administration, the Challenger explosion … the invention of the iPhone, had cooled the first flames of enthusiasm she'd felt, but in a good way. Like banking a fire, keeping the heat of it in the coals so it wouldn't take more than a little fuel — a stick and a puff of breath — for it to burst back into flame again.

There was nothing wrong with Willa Hannacker's life the way it was. Oh, the whole world had been turned upside down and wrong side out by the pandemic, and even though nobody talked about it, she knew other members of the family were really struggling with the repercussions of the shutdowns. But farming didn't shut down, she didn't have to wear a mask or concern herself with social distancing from the cows. She'd fared better than a whole lot of other people. And she'd met Isaiah. Isaiah who might be … drum-roll please … *the one.* Maybe. the possibilities of that set her whole body tingling.

The tragedy of Jessie's death still weighed heavily on the family, of course. She'd loved the woman dearly, everybody did. And today, Jessie'd whispered in Ruth's ear from the grave, revealed an incredible secret. And the wonder, the excitement … the possibility of adventure in that secret set every nerve in Willa's body tingling.

Listening to Ruth outline the possibilities of that secret, and describe the potential, Willa found the banked fire of her begin to glow brighter and hotter. The two of them had stumbled onto a gold mine, and the more Ruth talked the more convinced Willa became that it would be not just foolish … but wrong, in some fundamental way she couldn't have defined … to throw away the opportunity that lay before them.

It was clear, though, that her father and grandfather didn't share their offsprings' enthusiasm. She watched her father's face without appearing to stare, considered how his whole world had been shaped by the Cornbread Mafia. The greatest traumas in Drew Hannacker's life had been because of it. Witnessing his own grandfather's murder, watching his father's revenge on the murderer. His father suddenly locked in a cage for two decades, everything his family owned — from his mother's Mercedes to his own Big Wheel — snatched away by the government.

No, not everything. Not Coco. He'd kept the little foal, and it had given back to him the life, the hope and the future that marijuana had stolen.

AS DREW HANNACKER listened to his half-sister Ruth wax eloquent about the possibilities of a whole new future for the family, stored away in Mason jars in a tanker buried in a field, he found himself thinking about Coco.

That little horse had saved him. Drew knew that, understood it in a way nobody else possibly could. Everything the crumbling of the Cornbread Mafia empire had destroyed, the appaloosa foal had returned to Drew tenfold. Perhaps the brilliance of that one shining light of hope and life might not have shone so brightly if it hadn't been cast on the backdrop of a world that had been plunged into absolute darkness.

Drew's father had given him the horse for his ninth birthday, told him he could pick any one of the four foals at Land's End stables that day. But there'd been nothing for Drew to decide — the foal Coco picked him. He was slightly larger than the other three. His head and neck were a chocolate brown, though his mane and tail were black and he had a white mask on his face. From his shoulders back was white with gray, black and brown splotches and spots. His front legs were brown, like his neck. His back legs were brown, too, from the rump down. Coco had nudged the other three foals out of his way and approached Drew boldly, dropped his head and nickered softly. Then he'd put his velvet nose against Drew's cheek … and *whispered* to him.

At least, that's the way Drew liked to believe it'd happened. He liked to think that at that moment, he'd discovered his gift: Drew Hannacker was a horse whisperer.

That's what people called it when a trainer had the rare ability to … to *communicate* with a horse. From that moment forward, Drew had devoted his life to thoroughbreds, dropped out of the University of Kentucky after his junior year when he landed a job mucking out stalls at Calumet Farms in Lexington. He hadn't even turned thirty when the famous horse farm was forced at the last minute to scratch its entry in that year's Derby. They'd done some fast shuffling and replaced the horse with Doodlebug, a third-stringer that "showed promise," whose training had mostly been in the hands of a young trainer nobody'd ever heard of. The powers that be at Calumet Farms and the rest of the horse industry sat up and took notice when "Doodle-B," at 120-1 odds, came within a single length of standing in the winners' circle draped in a blanket of roses.

Drew's skill with horses was matched by a business acumen nobody would ever have supposed. For three decades, he trained some of the finest race horses in the state and then made a daring move that'd surprised the thoroughbred world. In 2019, when the on-its-last-leg horse farm called Land's End finally landed in bankruptcy court, Drew had pulled together a group of small investors and bought it, became the CEO of the corporation and managed the business.

He'd been making a go of it, could see a bright future out there on the horizon … until COVID transformed the sporting landscape. The NBA, the NHL, Major League Baseball and NASCAR suspended competition, the NCAA canceled all of its championships, the Masters golf tournament was postponed and for the first time in seventy-five years, the 2020 Kentucky Derby was not held on the first Saturday in May. The Kentucky equine industry was knocked to its knees that year, and struggled to regain its footing in 2021.

Drew had been staggered along with everybody else. And now, in the spring of 2022, the outlook for Land's End horse farm was not good. Thoroughbred races were segregated into age categories, and in the eyes of thoroughbred racing, all horses have the same birthday — January 1. So, if you were a baby horse born in February, you became one year old on January 1. If you were born in May, you become one year old on January 1. If you were born at 11:55 p.m. on December 31, you became one year old on January 1. Consequently, mare owners, a generally obsessive group of individuals, always tried to get an early start on the competition during breeding season — February 1 to July 4. You wanted yours to be the oldest, biggest and strongest horse on the field, not the youngest, smallest and weakest. Thoroughbred offspring had to be the result of a "live cover" mating — no sperm donors need apply. Drew Hannacker hadn't yet bred any of his mares, and the clock was ticking.

Stud fees were the issue. In his current financial position, Drew couldn't afford the stud fees — at least not for the horses with the kind of bloodlines he was looking for. Before he'd left the house this afternoon, he'd been studying the printout sof the Spendthrift Farms stud fee schedule for its stable of twenty-five stallions. You could breed your mare to Saratoga winner Yaupon — for an introductory stud fee of thirty thousand dollars. Or the Florida Derby winner Curlin, for ten thousand dollars. But it would cost a quarter of a million dollars to purchase a bump-and-tickle session for your mare with Into Mischief.

As he listened to Ruth outline the possibilities, it felt a little like a life preserver had been tossed to him just as he was about to go under.

But … marijuana. Drew didn't, he *couldn't* embrace the idea. Neither could he dismiss the possibilities out of hand.

He glanced at his father's face, wondering what he was thinking about what Ruth was proposing. Papa would be the toughest nut to crack. Weed had taken Papa's grandfather, his best friend and twenty years of his life from him. Drew couldn't imagine what it would take to get Riley Hannacker to set sail on that ship again.

Chapter Thirteen

Ruth wanted this. Wanted it badly. It was the ultimate opportunity of a lifetime.

All through business school at Stanford, she was preparing herself to make it big, a millionaire many times over someday. She envisioned herself at the helm of a big corporation *that she had built from the ground up*, the CEO or CFO, and she had worked night and day to build her businesses, the line of boutique stores and antique shops. She loved the businesses, loved the work, loved watching them grow. She was so very, very proud of what she'd accomplished. But she understood that both of those enterprises were self-limiting. Oh, she supposed it was possible to open a Ruth's Stuff boutique in every city in America, but she was certain market saturation would stall the enterprise out. And there were only so many antiques to be had. Though she loved prowling through mom-and-pop stores, yard sales, going-out-of-business and estate auctions, she could see that at some point that business would top out, too.

That was fine. It was all part of the greater plan — to

maximize their potential, to use them as a platform to launch out into something she could scale. She'd build other businesses, using the first two corporations to launch a third. And a fourth.

But that's not how it'd worked out.

Chutes and Ladders.

When she was a little girl, she and Mama had spent hours playing that game — where a single misstep could send you from the top of the heap to the bottom of the barrel.

COVID had done that to Ruth.

No, not COVID. Not the virus. The idiotic, moronic, purely political government responses to the virus had sent her businesses into a tailspin as they had the businesses of countless thousands of other Americans.

Just two weeks to flatten the curve. Right.

She'd never seen herself as a violent person, but she genuinely believed if she could get her hands around the throat of whoever came up with that gigantic lie, she would cheerfully choke the life out of them and gladly suffer the consequences.

Lockdowns. Going out to purchase "pretty stuff" wasn't in the government's definition of essential travel. Social distancing — God how she hated that term! — was impossible in her small, cozy stores, and allowing one customer at a time into the building didn't provide enough income to keep the places afloat. The pathetic jokes of "stimulus money" and "relief funds" — too little and too late with rampant, multi-million-dollar corruption — provided neither relief nor stimulus, and one after another her stores closed. By the time the idiot governors in the states where she operated got their heads out of their asses and began to allow non-essential businesses to reopen, only a handful of her Has-Beens antique stores were still limping along. All of her Ruth's Stuff stores were on life support, and she could hear the beeping of the financial heart monitor — beep ... beep ... beep ... bzzzzzzz.

By Thanksgiving 2021, Ruth had directed her attorneys to begin drafting Chapter 11 bankruptcy filings. Not file them, just draft them. She could see no way out but to liquidate her assets, such as they were, and start all over. At the bottom.

The last conversation she'd had with her mother had been about that, as the two of them set the table and Papa carved the Thanksgiving chickens — five of them. Nobody in the family liked turkey.

Her mother'd been so encouraging. She'd pointed out that Ruth had done it once, built businesses from nothing to prosperous — she could do it again. And three weeks later, Mama was dead.

And then this morning, Ruth had opened a letter that began *"My precious Ruthie ..."* and the whole world turned upside down. If it hadn't been for Willa, Ruth would have gone scurrying around gathering up the cash boxes of golden eggs in The Treehouse without even noticing the goose that'd laid them. Righteous Weed seed. Stick those little babies in the ground, water them and — hopefully! — they would blossom into the Cornbread Mafia 2.0. No, not that exactly. What her forebears had done was *against the law.* What she was suggesting was *legal* ... sorta, kinda. At least it would be legal one day. She could already see, though, that it couldn't start out that way, not if they had to wait a year, maybe two to get a license.

Of course, Ruth Hannacker didn't give a fig newton about what the law dictated — suspected that worldview was welded snugly into every molecule of her DNA — but the others might, none of them out of respect for jurisprudence but some of them out of pure prudence. Papa and

Drew had paid dearly for their involvement with the Corn-bread Mafia. They'd need a powerful motivation to be willing to get back into the water.

She'd been trying to read her audience, but she'd never been very good at that sort of thing. Probably too self-absorbed to be attuned closely to what other people were thinking and feeling. She knew she had Willa on her side. But the others … and she was running out of steam.

Finally, she stopped talking, walked to the fire and picked up a poker, jabbed at a small log to push it closer to the center of the flames.

She turned back to face them.

"This is all I got. I didn't come prepared with a State of the Weed Address. I got up this morning expecting to call my attorneys in Chicago …" she paused, "and tell them to file bankruptcy papers on three of the six Ruth's Stuff stores there." Everybody was surprised by that admission, except maybe Papa, and either he was just still too emotionally fried to be reacting emotionally to anything, or he'd already figured out she was in financial trouble. "And then I saw a light at the end of the tunnel that might or might not be a train."

Might … or might not. Truth was, Ruth desperately wanted this opportunity to succeed, to make good on all those ambitious dreams about owning and operating her own financial … empire, but the truth still in the husk was that she knew absolutely nothing about running a cannabis company and had no desire to learn. She could learn, of course. *Would* learn. After all, this was an opportunity to make millions.

Her father spoke, his voice soft.

"It was in 1973 or '74, I think. Willie Ray, Jessie, Papa and me was working in a field, topping the weed, when Joe Joe come running out of the woods like his pants was on fire, hollerin' 'the law's in.'" When he paused, she watched the scene form in the air in front of him. "You've all heard the story, about how we bailed into the trees and Papa come back half an hour later toting three dead squirrels, claiming he didn't know there was any weed growing anywhere around there — he'd just gone squirrel hunting."

They all remembered the story.

"When I picked up Willie Ray that day, I could see his mind spinning around so fast his thoughts was like to catch his hair on fire like Joe Joe's pants. He'd come up with a plan — that we'd ought to harvest the weed before the law come back in the morning to bush-hog it, that we'd put out the word — 'If you want to make a year's pay in one night, come on out and fill your truck up with weed.' By the time the law got back the next morning, they wasn't nothing left in that field but crisscrossing tire tracks in the mud."

He turned to Ruth then. "Me and Willie Ray had got it all worked out in our heads before we ever picked up your mama. When she heard the plan, she pointed out it'd be a whole lot simpler and easier to throw in the towel and write that patch off, let the law have it. Other than messing with Willie Ray's hybrid schedule, it wasn't our only field."

When he paused, Ruth saw him conjure up her mother's face in his head.

"Then Jessie looked from me to Willie Ray and back to me. And she said, 'You just don't want the law to destroy it because *you don't want them to win.*'"

He turned back toward the fire and his voice was even softer. "But they did win. In the end, they won and we lost." He looked at Drew. "I lost watching you become a man." His gaze shifted to Ruth. "I lost your whole childhood." Back to the fire. "And I lost twenty years I could have spent loving my Jessie."

He didn't say anything else for so long the silence

dragged out. Ruth wondered if she should say something—

"The stakes are different now." Papa's voice was still low, but it was no longer soft. "What ain't changed is the winnin' and losin' part. We found out that … what starts out looking like winnin' sometimes ends up being losin' in the long run." He shook his head. "Trouble was, by the time we'd figured out that part we were … stuck." He paused for a beat. "Like the Tar Baby."

Maybe the others knew what he was talking about, but Ruth didn't have any idea.

He stood slowly. "This ain't just up to me." But, of course, it was. If he'd put his foot down, it would have been over. "We," he made a gesture that encompassed the four of them, "got to decide what we're gonna do 'bout them seeds and ain't but one way to do that. We gotta vote. Rocks in a box."

Chapter Fourteen

Jessie had kept the box, of course. It was one of her most prized possessions and everybody in the family knew what it was and what it had meant to the members of the Cornbread Mafia. Riley reached up to take the box off the mantle, grateful that the box had been such a special part of their lives, enough to earn a permanent home on the mantle in the farm house living room. It'd stayed there, hadn't been moved to the lake house, hadn't been among every other thing the two of them had owned — blown out of the world. As he lifted it down, the memory of that first time welled up in his mind, made his eyes swim with tears.

"ROCKS IN A BOX, ROCKS IN A BOX," *Willie Ray suddenly cries, leaps up and heads out to his truck, trailing, "I'll be right back," in the air behind him like a balloon attached to his shoe. They see him get something out from under the front seat, then bend over and pick something up off the ground, several different somethings.*

He comes back into the office and holds out a wooden box, about the size of a box of tissues. It's handmade, but there are no visible nail holes. The surface is smooth and flawless, a dark ebony color, and there is a hole in the lid about the size of a fifty-cent piece.

"This here's the box Andy made for me to keep my baseball cards in," he says in a heartbreakingly hollow voice. "He made it in shop class in junior high."

The lid is hinged and he opens the box and they see inside what he'd been picking up. Rocks. They're small, different sizes, some light colors, others dark.

He tries to smile then, but can't quite pull it off. "I found a horned toad in the woods one summer and wanted to keep it as a pet, so he helped me drill a hole in the top of the box to let it breathe." He pauses. "Mama found the box in the back of Andy's closet when she was cleaning out … after. She thought I'd want it. I use it now, keep joints in it."

He tries again to smile and gets fairly close.

"That danged toad died anyway." He holds out the box. "Everybody get yourself a white rock and a black rock." Jessie looks at him questioningly. "Okay, I know they ain't white and black — light and dark, work with me, people."

He passes the box around and when everyone has two rocks, he pours the rest of the rocks out on the floor and closes the lid on the empty box.

RILEY OPENED the box and saw that there was a selection of white and black — light and dark — rocks inside and he didn't know where they'd come from or how they'd ended up in the box. It had first been used in an "official capacity" almost half a century ago when Papa had brought to them the proposal by Mama Bert to become their business partner. He gritted his teeth. Riley never allowed himself to think about Mama Bert or even now — even after all these years — rank anger rose up in the back of his throat like bad coffee. Riley'd paid her back for murdering his grandfather, learned the awful lesson that getting revenge didn't lessen the pain of grief, didn't return his grandfather to him, didn't even bring the precious "closure" all them folks who hadn't never lost anybody they loved seemed to think was out there for the taking and would be a valuable thing when you did. The second time they'd used the box was the night the three of them had voted to kill Jackson McClusky for what he'd done in Vietnam. The first time, the box had been filled with white rocks after the voting. The second, all three rocks inside had been black.

He felt the weight of it in his hand for a moment, then poured all the rocks out onto the coffee table.

"You guys know the drill. Everybody pick up one white and one black."

Drew merely reached down and picked up two rocks. It was different for Ruth and Willa, though. He watched the two of them — and he could see that what they were doing was important to them, not just that they were deciding, but *how* they were deciding. Rocks in a box — like they were participating in some mystical ceremony. And maybe it was, sort of. Riley didn't let his mind wander off down that rabbit trail, but did allow himself to acknowledge that this "tradition" mattered in ways too deep for his poor old tired mind to fathom.

When everybody had picked up two rocks — one white and one black — Riley said, "This ain't complicated. If you think we ought to get back into the weed business — whatever that takes, and however them that's in charge thinks is best — put a white rock in the box. If you think we ought to divvy up the money in the Tree House and pour the contents of them seed jars into the Rolling Fork River, put in a black rock.

He handed the box to Drew. Drew turned his back on the others and shoved one of the rocks in his hand down into the hole. He handed the box to Willa, who did the same thing, then passed it on to Ruth, who voted and handed the box back to Riley.

When Riley took the box from Ruth it felt way heavier than it had felt when he'd first picked it up off the mantle, and then it'd had maybe a dozen rocks in it. Now, it held only three, soon to be four. He turned his back and stood, holding it, wishing he hadn't waited until the last minute to make up his mind what he'd ought to do.

He sighed.

Bottom line: Riley Hannacker didn't have a right to decide for all the young people in the room how they'd ought to live their lives. Like every other old man, every old *fool*, he believed he knew what was best — that he could look back down through the tunnel of all his life experiences and make a wiser decision than they could.

But there was an even more fundamental bottom line buried down under the first one: You can't make somebody else's mistakes for them. Everybody's got to do that their own selves.

He knew Drew was having financial difficulties, not the specifics, but he could probably make a pretty accurate guess. He had *not* known that Ruth was in the same boat. Wasn't surprising, of course. The China Virus — he still called it that because by God that's what it *was!* — had crapped in the world's punchbowl and wasn't hardly anybody around who hadn't got hurt by it some way or another.

He didn't know for lead pipe certain exactly where each one would come down on this — white rock or black — but he was pretty sure the only rock that was really in doubt was his.

Trouble was, he just flat-out could not shake the conviction that his determination not to meddle in his kids' affairs didn't mean he had to allow his offspring to do something he *knew* would not turn out the way they expected! He had to protect them, didn't he? This would *not* end well. Maybe he should just back off, wash his hands of the whole thing, let them do this on their own.

Jessie's voice whispered in his ear. *"We need to be there, not just for the kids but* with *them."*

Riley's heart stopped beating. He could hear a warm smile in her voice then. *"Promise me we'll always have some skin in the game."*

He selected the white rock and put it through the hole in the top of the box, certain that it was snuggling up in there alongside three other rocks the same color.

Turning around, he handed the box to Ruth.

"Dump it out. Let's see what we got."

She hesitated for a beat, then turned the box upside down and bumped out the contents on the coffee table.

Four white rocks. They all looked at the rocks and then at each other.

"So let it be written," Riley said. "So let it be done."

Chapter Fifteen

It didn't matter that the day dawned cold and wet, with rain seeping down onto the earth from pewter clouds. It wouldn't have mattered if there'd been a hurricane blowing through Callison County. That might have slowed Willa and Ruth down a bit, but they'd have gone out in it just the same. They couldn't wait until there was more accommodating weather to clear out the contents of the Tree House — which now seemed so exposed, somehow, sitting out there with nobody around. The fact that it'd remained untouched for four decades should have been comforting, but that didn't seem enough anymore. Neither of the women would rest until the treasure from the Tree House was where they could keep their eyes on it.

And besides — the big question, the question of the century — will the seed grow? — couldn't be answered until they could bring it back to the house to see.

They set out right after breakfast. Neither of them had slept well the night before, their minds too full, racing, thoughts popcorning in their brains that kept them too agitated to sleep.

Ruth had lain awake in the darkness, trying to keep her emotions in check, but seeing a future out there within her grasp that could fulfill her lifelong dreams. Could she manage a cannabis company? And the management of the enterprise would fall to her, she was sure. Of course she could! There was so much to learn first, of course. So much to know that she didn't. Willa and Papa would have to be charged with the actual production of the product they'd be selling, but all the rest would be Ruth's baby. Anticipation kept her squirming around, unable to get comfortable for the rest of the night.

Willa drove as Ruth sat beside her in Willa's old truck, both of them watching the road blur and then become clear in rhythm with the wipers' course across the windshield. Willa intended to transfer the seeds from the six-quart Mason jars into zip-lock bags that she could carry out in a backpack, each of them faithfully labeled just as Willie Ray had done. His meticulous records would go into their own gallon zip-lock bag. Ruth figured the easiest, simplest way to transport the money was to dump the contents of the cash boxes into a garbage bag and haul it out over her back like Santa Claus.

"Did you get in touch with Isaiah last night?" Ruth asked.

"Uh huh," Willa said.

"And ...?"

"And I didn't tell him about it, if that's what you're asking."

"You didn't tell—?"

"Not over the phone. I want to do it face to face. I'll see him soon, sometime next week."

"You didn't mention it, so ... what? You just chatted amicably about ... oh, I don't know. How the Pirates look in spring training? Third Pass's odds in the Derby? The new orange mocha flavor at Starbucks?"

"Of course I wanted to say something. But … would you deliver that kind of news over the phone? 'Oh, by the way, I'm about to make millions of dollars, but I have to become a criminal—"

"Not criminal, law-breaker." It had become clear even in the brief discussion they'd had last night after the vote that nobody was in favor of trying to get a cannabis license somewhere to grow it legally. If they did, it'd be a year, likely longer, before they could see any return. They each had their own reasons for not wanting to wait, from simple eagerness to financial necessity. Oh, they would grow it legally as soon as they could, but bringing in a crop was the first priority — if for no other reason than to get a patent on the plant before they grew it commercially, out in the open.

"Same thing," Willa responded.

"No it isn't."

"It could be to Isaiah."

"Ya think?"

"No. Well, yeah. Maybe. He's an attorney."

"He's a corporate attorney. The law doesn't matter to those guys."

Willa shot her a withering look.

"I'm serious. I don't know how much he cares about … if he'll be offended or upset or afraid or …"

"And if he is?"

Willa was silent.

"I'll cross that bridge when I get to it. He knows something's up, though, could tell by my voice."

The rain had let up by the time they parked the truck beside the big chunk of rock that had fallen down next to the road, but the ground was wet and muddy and it was a challenge to make their way up the side of the knob to the not-a-meadow-anymore where the boulder pile lay.

Once inside the Tree House cavern, the actual gathering up of treasure didn't take long. Willa held open the garbage bag and Ruth dumped the contents from one after another of the cash boxes into it, then stacked the empty boxes back on the shelf.

Willa sealed Willie Ray's ledgers in a zip-lock bag and stuffed the bag into the bottom of her nylon, zippered backpack. Then she and Ruth carefully poured the contents of each Mason jar into its own labeled zip-lock bag. They only spilled a little on the floor.

The rain had started again by the time they'd packed up, and climbing up the wet rocks that hid the Tree House entrance was treacherous. The mud at the edge of the not-meadow beyond the boulders was so slick Willa's feet went out from under her and she landed with a splat on her backside. Ruth almost lost her footing several times on the hillside beyond and both of them were grateful to get back to the dry interior of the truck, where Willa quickly started the engine and cranked the heat.

Before she pulled away, her phone dinged with a text. She read it and looked up at Ruth.

"Guess Isaiah's more intuitive than I imagined. He's cancelled some Friday meetings and will be in Louisville for the weekend."

"Showtime."

Chapter Sixteen

"Stop hovering!"

Ruth had returned to lean over the plastic bag resting in the sunlight on the windowsill for the umpteenth time that morning, and she stood up in surprise when Willa spoke, banging her head on the open cabinet door.

"Ouch!" Rubbing the raw spot as Willa came up beside her to examine the contents of the bag, Ruth told her, "I'm not hovering!"

"You are, too."

"I am not." She rubbed her sore head.

"Are, too."

"Am *not!*"

"Are—"

"So what if I am. What difference does it make?"

"I told you — it won't grow if you keep hovering over it."

"Watched pot never boils? Seriously?"

Willa drew herself up to her full five feet, six inches — still six inches shorter than Ruth — and said solemnly,

"Not myth, science. Plants have feelings. Look it up if you don't believe me."

"And I'm ... what? Upsetting the seeds by looking at them?"

Willa nodded. "Yup. It is a proven scientific fact that if you stare at seeds, they flat-out will not germinate."

"Proven by whom?"

"By the Happy Clappy What's Happenin' Now School of Botanical Science and Chinese Carry-out Deli, that's who."

Willa turned away from the window, opened the refrigerator door and started rummaging around in it.

"I know there's some leftover broccoli-tomato hummus in here somewhere. You didn't eat it, didja?" That girl was like a hummingbird. She could eat everybody in the family under the table and never gained an ounce. Willa continued without waiting for a reply. "Wasn't Papa. I tried to get him to try it, but he swore off all my food recommendations after the vegetable smoothie, said it looked like what he cleaned out of the bottom of the lawnmower after he'd mown wet grass." She moved a jar of tahini and spotted the dish. "Here it—"

Suddenly, Ruth's breath caught in her throat. "There's something here, Willa."

"It's just your imagi—"

"No, it's real. I swear. Look."

Ruth backed away to give Willa room to peer at the baggie. Clearly her young cousin was not nearly as tense about the germination of the Righteous Weed seeds as Ruth was. So much ... so very much in Ruth's life was riding on this.

She'd joined in all the general discussions of how they should grow the weed crop, where, when and how much.

But for the more specific aspects of the process, all eyes turned to Willa and Dad.

Even after all their assurances, Ruth was still fearful that they were chasing a mirage. That after forty-three years in the dark of the Tree House, the Righteous Weed seeds had … petrified or something, died inside, whatever — some critical malady that meant they'd never germinate and grow. As soon as they returned to the farm with the contents of the Tree House, Willa had spent a day going over the ledgers Willie Ray had left behind, tracing the line — what he had bred to what — to get the Righteous Weed seed. There were several different iterations of the last plants Willie Ray'd been tinkering with when they got busted. He'd made slightly different hybrids for the different growing locations, and Willa wanted to start — this first crop — using the one most likely to grow well in the Kentucky climate.

That evening, Ruth watched Willa pour out some of the seeds from a zip-lock bag marked WI3-2K into a small bowl. It was the first time she'd gotten a good look at marijuana seeds. A little smaller than dried pinto beans, each seed was different, like picking up pretty shells on a beach. Pinto beans were blotchy, like somebody'd splattered brown paint on a pinkish-tan seed. Marijuana seeds were golden — not gold as a chickpea, more golden-brown, and the markings on them were patterns, like a terrapin shell or cracked dirt where a puddle had dried up.

"They're … striped," Ruth had said in awe. "Are all marijuana seeds striped?"

"Naaa, and Willie Ray said Wazzi didn't know why they'd come out looking like that," Papa had said. "Over the years, Willie Ray and Wazzi worked with all kinds of different seeds, different sizes, shapes and colors — little bitty black ones from Thailand, dark brown ones from

New Zealand, grayish-brown ones from Florida that had tiger stripes, and golden ones from California. Willie Ray's cross-breeding produced patterned/striped seed that grew Righteous Weed." Her father paused again, and his eyes had a distant look. 'Willie Ray always said Righteous Weed 'smoked so smooth it was like you was breathing the mist hanging over a creek on a spring morning.'"

Willa'd dampened a couple of paper towels, put four or five of the seeds inside the towel, placed it in a baggie and placed the baggie on the windowsill, in the warm sunlight. "Now, we wait."

That'd been three days ago, and Ruth had to admit that Willa was right, Ruth *had* been obsessing over the seeds, checking every couple of hours to see if anything had happened. No change. Until today.

Willa picked up the baggie and peered into it. Ruth had not dared to touch it, afraid if she did — like her mother'd talked about tiptoeing around the kitchen when there was a cake in the oven … or it would "fall."

"See, right there," Ruth prompted. "The green poking out of the shell of that one."

"Your eyesight's better than mine," Willa said, and Ruth's stomach fell. "But yeah, I see it, the shell has cracked on one and its growing." She held up a fist for a fist bump. "Houston, we have liftoff."

"What about the others?"

"Somebody's always gotta be first. The others will sprout, too, you'll see. Or maybe this is the only seed in the whole bag that will germinate." She must have seen the stricken look on Ruth's face because she cried, "Chill! Joke. You grew up on a farm! You know you never get all the seeds of anything to germinate — but I'm betting the rest of these are just as eager to get out of those shells as this fella is."

Willa popped the germinated seed into a small pot with good potting soil, just lay the seed on top and lightly sprinkled potting soil over it. Veeeery shallow. Then she spritzed the soil with water a couple of times and sealed the pot in a larger plastic bag and put it back in the window.

Ruth had said nothing during the process, just watched. Willa straightened after setting the bag back on the window sill.

"That's it, then," Ruth said, the hollow place of fear/dread/pessimism filled now with an equally uncomfortable hollow place bubbling with anticipation.

Willa lifted her phone and took a picture of the baggie on the windowsill. "I think we should call her Phoebe."

"Her?"

"Anything as important in your life as what could make you a millionaire ought to have a name, don't you think?"

"But *Phoebe*?"

"Yeah, well, no sense wasting a good name on a plant." She paused. "I'll show her picture to Isaiah tomorrow."

"What do you think he'll say?"

"… probably that she has my eyes."

Chapter Seventeen

Drew came over that night to meet with the other members of CBM2, as Willa had taken to calling the four of them, since the "birth" of Phoebe that afternoon had made it clear their enterprise was more than just a pipe dream. He brought a pot roast Andrea'd had in the oven all day.

As Ruth filled glasses with ice, Drew described the conversations he'd had with Andrea and with Willa's sister, Lissa.

"Truth is, Andrea is not happy about this," he said. "She's scared it's all going to blow up in our faces. "

"And Lissa?" Riley asked.

"You know Lissy. If it's what the rest of us want …"

"How about Joel?" Ruth asked.

"He's pretty freaked, too," Drew admitted. "You can't blame him — four kids and one on the way. If we got busted—"

"How about we put that one to bed once and for all," Riley said, his voice stern. "Nobody's getting busted. This enterprise is going to be in the wind for six or eight months, and after that we do it by the book. We're going to tippy-toe outside the law and then leap back inside again so fast ain't nobody even gonna notice we was missing."

He took a breath. "If the guano does come in contact with the air-conditioning during that time — and it won't! — but if it does, it will go down just like it did forty years ago. I'll take the fall."

Everybody tried to talk at once then, but Riley banged his fist down on the table and the group fell into shocked silence. None of them had ever seen their father/grandfather like this. Ruth considered that he had buried this man deep inside when he got out of federal prison and the Riley he'd once been was making an appearance for the first time since.

"We will *never* have this conversation again — is that understood?" Silence. "I am seventy-two years old and I've had a good life. I have seen prison and nobody I love will ever set foot inside one. We clear on that?" He looked into the eyes of each before he continued. "None of you has anything to worry about! And you can't do this if you're scared. When you scared, you look scared and act scared and eventually folks start to wonder what it is you so afraid of. We ain't got nothin' to be scared of 'cause we ain't doin' nothing wrong." It almost sounded like he ground his teeth. "It being illegal don't make it *wrong.* You hold your head up high, go on about your life like ain't nothing changed. This family is going to be just fine."

Maybe *fine,* but not the *same.* The family was different already because each of them had changed in response to the treasure they'd found. Subtle changes, mostly. There was a sparkle in Drew's eyes, like maybe the future he saw in the tomorrows stacked one on top of the other out there in the mist had been altered. Willa was ... well, *Willa,* but industrial-strength Willa, Willa-squared, so full of energy/excitement/anticipation she almost glowed. The treasure had pulled Ruth out of a very dark place, where constant worry about her businesses had collided with grief over her mother's death. But Papa, this side of Papa. What she and Willa had found in the Tree House had called him forth, like rubbing the side of a bottle and up pops a genie. This was the man created by his first encounter with illegal weed. None of them had ever met this man.

No one spoke then.

Well, except Willa. After an uncomfortable silence, she said, "Am I the only one here who feels like they just got trampled by a herd of stampeding rhinos wearing football cleats?" Ruth watched a look pass over her father's face … was it gratitude that his granddaughter had put the cork back in the bottle? Or maybe just remembrance. Willa held out her plate. "Give me some of that pot roast before I bleed out."

His point made, Papa retreated into the shell he'd inhabited since Mama died, participated in the conversation when his input was solicited, but otherwise just observed.

Papa, of course, would have picked growing the crop outside. That was what he knew, but he acknowledged that times and circumstances had changed.

"You saying we grow it inside somewhere, under lights and all that?" he asked Willa.

"Uh huh."

"So we'd have to buy equipment, set it up, operate and maintain it?"

"There's enough money in the cash boxes to fund set-up and marketing," Ruth said.

"Last I checked, sunshine's free."

"Yeah, Papa, but it doesn't have an off/on switch. And

Willa says with adjustments to the lights that are pretending to be the sun, you can fool the plants into growing and maturing faster."

"Plants are that stupid, you think?"

She nodded.

"So we buy them grow lights? Where?"

"I can arrange that," Willa said.

"I have lots of lawyers that I owe a lot of money," Ruth said. "Their meters are always running, so I'll get them to set up half a dozen shell corporations, buy equipment in three or four different places so it's not traceable."

"Growing them inside, we can baby every plant, pamper each one, give them a balanced diet," Willa said. "No Twinkies or Ho Hos or Moon Pies."

"And you have a place all picked out?"

"I have a likely candidate in mind," Drew said, and Ruth saw her grandfather make the connection. The horse barn where they'd processed thousands of pounds of marijuana for five years on the back side of Land's End was still there and it was currently sitting empty. They had gutted the barn fifty years ago, taking out all the stalls and installing long tables, with comfortable chairs where they'd sit for hour after hour, trimming marijuana buds by hand.

Roughly forty feet by eighty feet, the barn hadn't been left totally unused for the past four decades. After Malcolm Murdock's estate sold the place to Wainwright Stables, Herb Wainwright renovated all the barns. He didn't use that one to house horses since all the stalls had been removed. Instead, he transformed the hollow structure into a show ring, a place where his three children could train and then show their Tennessee walking horses. Land's End farm had become quite well known for walking horses for a couple of decades until Drew and his company bought it and he set his sights on making it a first-class thoroughbred farm.

The barn had fallen into some disrepair, the old boards bleached to a smooth mat gray by the sun. But that was the good news, the girls said, because it was good camouflage. The structure sat off by itself on a hillside on the back of the farm and a good-sized stand of trees had grown up around it. The road that'd been used to take horses back and forth to the show ring from the barns and paddocks on the farm hadn't been used in years and was overgrown with weeds, Queen Anne's lace, thistles and brambles. A trail you couldn't see unless you knew it was there snaked off Middleton Road on the other side of the knob from the farm and came out in the trees behind the barn, and that was the road the Cornbread Mafia workers had used before, the road CBM2 would use to haul in equipment — lights and grow tents and potting soil.

"If we run them grow lights twenty-four-seven, don't you think maybe somebody's gonna notice the electricity usage?" Papa asked.

"I'm planning to have a talk with Ralph at RECC," Drew said. Rural Electric Cooperative Company provided power to Callison and several other rural Kentucky counties. "I'll tell him we're installing big fans in all the barns, plan to run them around the clock for a season to see if cooler temperatures and better air flow makes for happier ponies."

"You think he'll buy that?"

"Everybody knows thoroughbred breeders have money to burn."

"We'll get a big, heavy-duty gasoline-powered generator that we can use if the power goes out," Willa said.

After the supper dishes were cleared away, the four sat

around the table, going over Ruth's business model and Willa's growing schedule.

They would set up inside the barn a dozen ten-by-ten-foot indoor grow tents — double rows of six in the center of the building with an aisle down between them and space on all sides between the island of tents and the building's walls. They would store supplies there — potting soil, white gallon buckets for the seedlings, bags of fertilizer, a big water tank set on a six-foot stand to provide water pressure. Each of the grow tents could house up to twenty-five plants.

"We're shooting for two hundred-fifty plants, going for a yield of half a pound to a pound of weed from each, with a sale price of four thousand dollars a pound," Ruth said. The numbers weren't a surprise to anybody, but it was still a conversation stopper to put them out there in a working plan. "A hundred twenty plants will gross a quarter to half a million dollars. If all two hundred-fifty plants make it, that's half a million to a million dollars."

She let that lie, then continued. "With that kind of working capital, we can get a grow license and/or dispensary licenses for next year, buy land to grow it outside or property for inside in most of the legal states. By then," she looked at Willa, "we'll have a patent and we'll be ready to rumble."

"We'll have a product to sell before Christmas this year," Willa said, then rattled off the growth stages — seedlings for two weeks, mid to late April, vegetative stage for four weeks, flower for eight to twelve weeks, which would put them into mid-July to mid-August. If the plants matured as planned, they'd harvest it in September, but that was just a target date. They wouldn't cut it until it was ready to be cut, until the colas were ripe. Then they'd dry it for two weeks and cure it for … "however long we decide to cure it."

"The longer you cure it, the more potent it is," Ruth put in. "That's what our botanist-in-residence tells me."

"Righteous Weed is … a bit of an unknown, from a purely botanical perspective," Willa continued. "There's all kinds of information about, say Michoacan Sativa, or the southeast Asian strains grown in Hawaii, or Mullumbimby Madness from Australia and Haze from Central America. In general terms, we know that Indica marijuana grows faster than Sativa and is skinnier and taller. Sativa bushes out more, the plants are short and fat."

She paused.

"But Righteous Weed isn't any of those, so …"

"The limbs are spaced far apart on the stem — Willie Ray bred for that so there was plenty of room for fat colas," Riley said. "But it can get away from you, grow taller than you wish it was. When you're hiding it behind corn, you have to be careful to keep it topped, or you'll end up having to bend some of the plants over and tie them to the ground so they can't be seen. Them grow lights and them tents—"

"The tents are expandable and we'll space them plenty far apart," Willa said. "We'll keep the lights suspended only a few feet above the plants and move them up as the plants get bigger."

"Basically, we'll just have to fly the plane while we're building it," Ruth said.

"Figure it out as we go along," Willa said. The warm glow of excitement and anticipation on her face would have melted frost off a window pane in an igloo.

Chapter Eighteen

Willa stayed at the airport until Isaiah's plane took off. She'd brought him to the departure doors and dropped him off out front. She'd watched him walk into the building, his back straight, strides long. He never looked back.

When she was sure he'd gone through security and was on the other side, she went into the building, found a seat where she could see the runways through the floor-to-ceiling windows. And she sat there while little kids climbed into the lap of the larger-than-life Colonel Sanders statue in front of the Kentucky Fried Chicken mini-restaurant.

It wasn't really that she thought/hoped he might call. That he'd have a sudden change of heart. That he'd say he was sorry, he hadn't meant to be so rigid and unyielding, that he hadn't intended to be "wrapped so tight."

He wouldn't do that. She was sure he wouldn't.

But she couldn't leave until he was gone. When that plane lifted off the tarmac and leapt into the sky, it was over. No last-minute reprieve. No running into his arms when he came back out into the lobby looking for her.

No I'm-sorrys. No it's-okays. No please-forgive-mes.

It was done.

When the plane was no longer even a black speck in the sky, Willa turned from the spot where she'd had her nose pressed to the glass and walked slowly out to the parking garage to her truck. She sat behind the wheel for a long time, wanting to cry, needing to cry, but unable to find tears for a pain she never dreamed would be so eviscerating.

And the thing was, she hadn't even realized that she loved him, *how much* she loved him, until she'd lost him.

She shouldn't have blurted the whole thing out as soon as he got into her truck, should have waited, let their joy at seeing each other set the tone for the conversation. But no, Willa had plowed into it before they were out of the airport parking lot, had unloaded a considerable amount of family history, and begun the exciting tale of her past week as they were pulling into the parking lot of the Cracker Barrel Restaurant on Crittendon Drive, near the airport. They never even got out of the truck.

At first, he'd thought she was making the whole thing up and made fun of her. That was infuriating.

"... a treasure chest buried in a field? Was there a dead body buried with it? Pirates always—"

"That's not what I said. You're not listening."

"You said there was buried treasure—"

"The word treasure was figurative, not literal. That's just what it seemed like. I mean ... a propane tanker in a cave ... money boxes on shelves with bills stuffed in them. It *felt* like finding a buried treasure."

She couldn't manage to get the conversation back on the rails after that. It seemed like he was determined to take everything she said the wrong way.

He'd called the money "dirty money," and when she'd taken umbrage at that, he'd asked what the proper terminology was for "money made illegally and hidden in the ground by criminals."

She'd said they weren't criminals.

He'd said that was the definition of people who broke the law.

She never should have mentioned the seed after that. She should have seen his reaction coming a mile out, but she'd been so determined to make him *understand.* She'd thought if she could just explain it properly, he'd get it — that they were just farmers and …

"You're not seriously considering doing this, are you, Willa? Do you know what the penalty is for—"

She lost it then.

"I know what the penalty is a helluva lot better than you do. I know the penalty up close and personal. My grandfather rotted away in a maximum security prison for two decades because he dared to commit the crime of criminal farming."

"Riley Hannacker was the mastermind of a multi-million-dollar illegal drug empire."

"Riley Hannacker was a farmer who grew his first crop of weed to keep his brain-damaged war buddy out of a VA hospital."

"He made millions."

"Selling weed — and where, pray tell, is the victim of that heinous crime?"

"That's just how it starts."

"Please! You're not really going there, are you? My grandfather went to prison for something that's not even a crime anymore in eleven states. You know as well as I do that in five years marijuana will be legal all over the country."

"Oh, I misunderstood. I didn't get the part where you

said you're planning to wait five years until it's *legal* to grow it in Kentucky."

"We *will* grow it legally. We *will* get a license. But we have to grow it in a barn here first so we can get a patent or somebody could steal it."

"And that'd be a shame, wouldn't it, for some thief to come along and steal your illegal marijuana."

It had gone on and on like that. Well, not just like that. He'd told her he was afraid for her. Didn't say the L-word. Didn't say he loved her. Just said he was afraid something terrible was going to happen to her. That he cared. That he didn't want her to get hurt.

He said that, as he hurt her worse than she had ever been hurt in her life. At some point, she'd realized it was hopeless. Somewhere inside, she understood that the Callison County cultural view of the law had soaked into her DNA when she wasn't looking. Her grandfather's generation had distrusted the law, then disrespected it and in the end disregarded it completely. She didn't necessarily feel that way about all law, but what the supremely unfair laws regarding marijuana had done to her family was irreparable harm. You couldn't be on the receiving end of that kind of injustice without it altering your views on life.

Eventually, they'd both worn down. Irresistible force, immovable object — that kind of thing. They both recognized it for what it was. While she was in the restaurant using the bathroom, he'd placed a call and snagged a standby seat on a flight leaving Louisville International Airport for Atlanta in ninety minutes. There'd be a three-hour layover at Harts-field International, but Isaiah said he didn't mind, wordlessly got out of her truck and retrieved the bag he'd placed in the back a two-hour lifetime ago ... and walked out of Willa's life.

Reaching up, she felt how wet her cheeks were and

assumed she must have been crying, but she hadn't been aware of it. She hadn't been aware of anything except the gigantic hole in her belly that ached in rhythm with the beat of her heart.

Papa and Ruth weren't expecting her back home tonight so the house was black and silent when she pulled into the driveway and let herself in the kitchen door.

As she slipped through the house toward the stairs, she chanced to glance into the living room. There was Papa, sitting in the darkness, staring at nothing, totally unaware of her presence.

For the first time, she had just an inkling of what he must have been feeling.

Chapter Nineteen

"… not going to dig it up because it's a *righteous* weed," Chase told Luna. At least that's what Sherry Lynn thought the little boy had said. She must have misunderstood. The two children were playing in the area of bare dirt beside the back porch of the cottage where Sherry Lynn was staying at Land's End. It hadn't always been bare dirt — there'd been tomato plants growing there once. Then the plants vanished. There, then gone. Poof. Magic. Sherry Lynn had asked the man who owned the house — he looked familiar but she couldn't recall his name — what happened to the tomato plants and he said *she* had pulled them out of the ground by the roots! She'd never heard anything as preposterous in all her life. Why would Sherry Lynn have done such a thing? Clearly, it was as she had feared. Riley had found her again! He'd found her and come after her, just like he did every time she tried to get free. He'd send that FBI agent to get her, handcuff her and haul her away, throw her out on the street with nothing but the clothes on her back. Riley wanted to make her a beggar, while he and *that woman* lived in Sherry Lynn's beautiful mansion with all Sherry Lynn's beautiful things.

It broke Sherry Lynn's heart to see it, to see what *his father* and *that woman* had done to poor little Drew. Riley had stolen everything from his wife and son — their beautiful home and sports cars and clothes and pretty things — took it all and gave it to *that woman*.

"… 'sposed to be digging up weeds — Grandma Sher said," the little girl called Luna told the little boy. Who names a little girl *Luna*?

"Not the righteous weeds!" the little boy said.

Righteous weed. Why would the child use that term? Sherry Lynn concentrated on what the children were saying, tried to turn up the volume on her hearing aid so she could hear, but by the time she found the right button, the children were prattling away about something else entirely. It was hot and Sherry Lynn did *not* like to sweat. When she was a child, she had thought it was so unbecoming to see big sweat rings under the arms of the old ladies at church, like they had never heard of deodorant and antiperspirants. She shook her head. Now that she was the little old lady instead of the little girl, she understood. Old people sweat *all over*. She could feel a stream of it sliding down between her pendulous breasts, and a bright blossom of it spreading out across the back of her shirt. And you couldn't smear deodorant all over your whole body.

She rocked slower, fanned herself more vigorously, curtaining her hand over her eyes as she peered down the road for the plume of dust that would announce Lissa had come to pick up the children. Lissa … her granddaughter. That's right. And the children were … her great grandchildren. That was impossible. Sherry Lynn was too young to have great grandchildren. She was only … she was seventy-two. How could …?

If Drew and Andrea hadn't gotten married right out of high school and had Willa and Lissa right away, and if Lissa hadn't started popping out offspring like rabbits as soon as she got married, Sherry Lynn wouldn't still be chasing toddlers around on her arthritic knees. At least Lissa had taken the two youngest with her to the grocery store this afternoon. The screeching of the little one, McKenna, made Sherry Lynn's hearing aid buzz and pop.

When she let herself think about it — and she didn't do that often — Sherry Lynn had to admit she hadn't been much of a grandparent to Willa and Lissa because when they'd come along, she'd been married to Tim Brand and he had those three little hellions. Not quiet and polite like Drew had been — those boys had been serial killer wannabes when they were still in diapers. And, of course, she and Tim weren't raising them in a mansion with two Olympic-sized swimming pools. Oh, they had a pool, above-ground, in the back yard. It leaked and the boys were always tracking mud into the house so Sherry Lynn tried to make Tim get rid of the pool. There's been a big blowup when he refused, and then he'd pitched a conniption fit when he came home after work and found her hosing the boys down before she'd let them in the house. What did he expect her to do, spend her life on her hands and knees cleaning up mud off the floor?

Benjamin Connelly's little girl had been much easier to deal with than Tim Brand's boys — until the girl turned thirteen and overnight became a world-class slut, wearing too much makeup and skimpy clothes. Sherry Lynn's father would have grounded her for the rest of her life if she'd tried to set one foot out the door in what that girl wore to school every day. Of course, Ben defended the little harlot, said all the girls dressed like that — which they did, but that didn't make it right! When Sherry Lynn caught the girl smoking, and her father said all the other girls did that, too, it was more than Sherry Lynn could stand, and so …

Sherry Lynn hadn't divorced her fourth husband, Clive McClusky. The priest had had to scurry around, trace down their family trees before he'd perform the ceremony — which wasn't an uncommon thing at all in Callison County. Turned out Clive's grandfather and Sherry Lynn's great-grandfather had been first cousins, or something like that. Clive had had no children so there'd been no step-children issues, and truthfully her marriage to him might have outlasted them all — if he hadn't collapsed in church from what they called a "widow-maker" heart attack before their tenth anniversary.

A bead of sweat dripped down out of Sherry Lynn's hair and ran down her temple. She'd had enough. She was going back in the house to the air conditioning.

"You kids gather up those tools and come on in — it's too hot out here."

"Mommy said we could play in the dirt," the little girl said, sticking out her lip.

Sherry Lynn pretended to look around. "Well, I don't see your mama anywhere so I guess you're going to have to do what I say."

Neither child made any movement to obey.

The little boy, Chase, was scraping a garden claw across the dirt, making designs.

"Would you like a bowl of ice cream?"

That got the little girl's attention. Sherry Lynn had no idea if there was ice cream in the kitchen, but all she had to do was get the kids inside and then they'd be Andrea's problem.

"Can we have ice-ceam even if we didn't get all the weeds?" she asked.

"You can't cut righteous weed," Chase said, sounding like a trying-to-be patient big brother. "It's a good weed 'cause Aunt Willa is growing it."

Though Sherry Lynn was still hot, she felt a chill down her spine, like there was ice water dripping slowly from one vertebra to the next.

Willa was growing Righteous Weed.

No, Sherry Lynn had to have misunderstood.

"Come on over here, Chase," Sherry Lynn said, "and tell your Grandma Sher why you don't want Luna to dig up those weeds."

"Aunt Willa came over yesterday to stay with us while Mommy went to the ob-ste … ob-ster-irician—"

"Obstetrician," Sherry Lynn finished impatiently.

"Yeah, that. And Aunt Willa was on her phone, on FaceTime with Aunt Ruth—"

"Ruth Monaghan is not your aunt!" Sherry Lynn snapped. She couldn't help herself. It made her skin crawl to hear Drew's children and grandchildren call *that woman's* daughter "Aunt." She was *not* their father's sister and her last name was *Monaghan*. Changing it to Hannacker when she got out of high school didn't mean a thing. Some judge saying she was a Hannacker didn't make her one.

The child shut up as if Sherry Lynn had scolded him and she realized how angry and hostile her voice had sounded. She painted sweetness and honey on it and back-tracked.

"I just meant she's not an *aunt,* sweetheart, she's a cousin or something, that's all. Like all your other cousins. Now, what was it she and Willa were saying about Right-eous Weed?"

"Aunt … *Cousin* Ruth said she hadn't seen the Righteous Weed in awhile and Aunt Willa said it was huge, that it was 'growing like a weed' and Aunt ... *Cousin* Ruth laughed."

"Righteous Weed." Sherry Lynn said the words aloud. "Is that what Willa said — you sure? Righteous Weed?"

The little boy nodded his head vigorously.

"But *this* isn't Right Just weed," Luna told him, indicating a scrawny plant that'd somehow survived the children's onslaught. "It's just a plain old weed. And you're s'posed to pull up weeds so the garden will grow."

The children then began to argue about weeds, how you could tell which ones to pull up and which ones not and Chase maintained that there couldn't be any righteous weed in Grandma Sher's garden because Aunt Willa was growing the weed on purpose in her *own garden.*

"Do you know where Aunt Willa's garden is?" Sherry Lynn asked the little boy.

Both children shook their heads.

Then Sherry Lynn saw on the road the plume of dust she'd so been looking forward to a few minutes before, which meant that Lissa was returning for the children. She didn't want the kids to tell their mother what they'd been talking about.

"Who knows the whole alphabet song?" she asked.

"I do!"

"I do!"

"A. B. C. D. E. F. G," Chase began to sing and his sister chimed in. "WXYG."

Sherry Lynn called out, "Lissy's here," to Andrea inside, who said she'd be "right out."

Lissa stopped in front of the house and left the younger children buckled up — and the air conditioner full on — as she got out to get the older two. She looked tired and frazzled ... that special kind of pregnant tired that came from sleep deprivation, never able to get comfortable in bed.

"There are suckers in a sack on the front seat," Lissy told the kids and the two of them almost knocked her down as they ran past. She turned to call after them, "Only one for each of you. No fighting."

Words leapt out of Sherry Lynn's mouth before she could stop them.

"Chase didn't want to pull up all the weeds. He said some of them were righteous weed."

She watched Lissy go rigid. She didn't turn around, just stood frozen for a few seconds, and when she did turn, her face was composed and "arranged," meaning she had pasted an inquisitive look on her features and was holding onto it with all her strength. She wouldn't look her grandmother in the eye.

"Wonder how he came up with a thing like that?"

It was true, then!

Holy shit. Her granddaughter Willa was growing weed — *marijuana!* — with ... with ... *that woman's* daughter, Ruth. The revelation was staggering, but Sherry Lynn was as certain as she'd ever been of anything in her life that it was true.

Andrea stepped out the front door then, wiping her hands on a dish towel. She looked from one of them to the other.

"Something wrong?" she asked.

"No," they both said with the perfect unison of a chorus line.

"We were just talking about how kids'll say anything," Sherry Lynn said.

"Won't they!" Lissy let out the breath she'd been holding and continued to babble, "just no telling what they'll come up with, is there?"

Then she hustled those kids into the car like they was about to catch on fire, told Andrea thanks for watching the kids, though it'd been Sherry Lynn who'd been keeping an eye on them outside. "See you Sunday," she said and almost threw driveway gravel out behind the back tires in her hurry to get gone.

Andrea stood looking mildly puzzled, turned like she was about to ask Sherry Lynn something, then thought better of it and just went back inside.

Sherry Lynn sank back down into the rocker. *That woman's* daughter and her precious Willa — mixed up in growing weed. Well, wasn't any way in the world Sherry Lynn was gonna sit by and let *that* happen.

Chapter Twenty

When Damien Coulter first saw the words "Righteous Weed" in the Facebook post for Baby Bear's Bed, Inc., he wrote it off as advertising hype. Righteous Weed, he thought. Riiiiight. And I got some swampland in Florida you might want to look at, too.

He completely forgot about it. Then he saw it again in the Twitter feed of Weed-R-US. And again on the PotheadsUnite Facebook page. Both fringe sites, of course. Still …

Now, there it was again, plain to see in *Cannabis Magazine* — right alongside cannabis news stories like "Smoking vs. Vaping Cannabis — What's the Difference?", "How to Prevent and Cure a Weed Hangover," "Cannabis Sales Broke Records During the Pandemic" and "Using Cannabis Is Morally Acceptable to 70 Percent of Americans."

The artwork was a huge marijuana leaf out of focus in the background. The foreground contained the question: "Want the same high you got that first time? Then smoke the same weed. If your first-time weed was *Righteous Weed*

… it's baaaaack. And the ONLY place to get Righteous Weed is here — BabyBearsBed.com."

He clicked on the link and the website made all kinds of claims that couldn't possibly be true.

The copy claimed that the company Baby Bear's Bed had found a buried treasure. A little like the Ark of the Covenant. Real, no-kidding Righteous Weed *seeds*. The originals, from forty years ago!

"And guess what — those babies will still grow. This fall will be the first harvest of that weed crop, and there will be only a limited amount available. If you want to be among those lucky customers, click here and sign up."

When you clicked to sign up, however, you were directed to a page where you could put your name on a waiting list! Smart advertising — create scarcity. Drives the price up.

Coulter didn't sign up. Instead, he told his assistant to set up a Zoom call ASAP with Moe, Curly and Larry. Half an hour later the CEO of CoulterCulture Cannabis, Inc., one of the three largest commercial cannabis companies in the country, was sitting in front of the seventy-five-inch big screen television in the conference room, looking into the faces of the three vice presidents he'd privately named after the Three Stooges.

Moe was Travis Dunn, a hawk-faced man with dark hair and eyes — surely got to claim a seat on the bus with the "I" group of LGBTQIA — indigenous people. If he wasn't Native American, he looked enough like one to fake it. And these days, claiming that kind of ancestry could land you a lot of perks. Just ask Elizabeth Warren. The background behind his face was a sunny beach and palm trees, but Coulter knew that was a virtual background he'd picked out, that he was actually sitting in his office in Orlando. Coulter would wager the company's pension fund that Dunn hadn't gotten sand between his toes a single time the whole ten years he'd lived in Florida.

Curly was Pete Clifford. His background was real — the big window behind his desk in his office in Colorado Springs looked out over a mountain vista stunning enough to inspire John Denver. Clifford was young and … what was it called? Not "upwardly mobile" anymore, something else. He had his eye on greater things than a vice presidency at CoulterCulture, and could be counted on to weigh every decision through the what's-in-it-for-me? lens of his own self-absorption. But he was smart — cagy, clever smart and that's why Coulter had hired him.

The background behind the talking head of the third vice president, Russell Brockawitz, was a blank wall. Could have been anywhere. If Coulter had to guess, he'd say "Larry" was in his living room in his house outside Muskogee, Oklahoma, dressed in a shirt and sports coat from the waist up and a pair of tighty-whities over black socks and house shoes from the waist down. He, among all the hierarchy of Coulter's company, had been the most determined to cling to the whole work-at-home environment fostered by the pandemic.

"This Righteous Weed shit is turning up like a bad penny everywhere I look," Coulter said. "What's up with it?"

"What's Righteous Weed?" Dunn asked.

"It claims to be weed from the 1970s," Brockawitz responded. Obviously, Dunn hadn't been surfing the web like Brockawitz had. If you sat home all day every day, what else was there to do?

"You want me to start tracking it down?" Clifford asked. "I'll put somebody on it."

"Only if there's anything to track down. It is a creative

advertising shtick, catering to the nostalgia of 'that first high,'" Brockawitz pointed out.

"I'm just wondering what kind of weed they're really hawking," Coulter said.

Obviously Dunn had just googled the words and was scrambling to get up to speed. "Says a company called Baby Bear's Bed is behind it."

"How do we know it's not three guys in their basement growing a single plant under a grow lamp?" Clifford offered.

"If it's three guys, it's three guys with 'means.'" Brockawitz pointed out. "Buying the kind of advertising they're putting out there costs serious change. Why would you go to that much expense if you didn't have something to sell that'd justify it? I signed up on the website—"

"All I got was a waiting list," Coulter said.

"I don't see a price here anywhere," Dunn said, obviously looking at the company's webpage. "Just a price range. They're going to be asking upwards of three K a pound. That's pretty ballsy for a brand new, out-of-nowhere company."

"I track every new product I come across and this one burst on the scene back in early June," said Brockawitz. He was that kind of nerd, would have dug into it, stayed up all night in his underwear scouring the internet for all the information he could find. "The first post I saw claimed there'd be 'samples available to potential buyers' this fall. Which tells me they don't have any inventory from last year's crop. Does that mean there wasn't a crop last year?"

That was a conversation stopper.

Coulter felt something grab hold of him deep in his belly. You didn't stand outside your ice cream stand handing out wooden spoonfuls of your product unless you knew it was good enough to get customers inside to buy.

"That's crazy," Dunn said.

Coulter agreed. It was like a runner nobody'd ever heard of winning the Boston Marathon. He was a runner, he knew — you could see good distance runners a long way out. If somebody was good enough to win the Boston Marathon, they'd been competing for a long time, working their way up. There were surprises, of course. People you didn't expect. But you could trace the history of runners back a long way. They didn't just burst full grown from an oak tree like Tecumseh. It was the same with good weed. You didn't get a hybrid that ticked all the boxes without a lot of trial and error. Mostly error — that's what you learned from. If these birds really did have great weed, it had taken them time — years, to perfect the strain. You didn't do that kind of thing in a vacuum.

"You don't suppose it's true, do you?" asked Clifford. "That they really got their hands on—?"

"On seeds for Righteous Weed?" Dunn interrupted. "Where could they get seed for a plant that hasn't been grown anywhere in forty years?"

"And even if they did — which they couldn't, but even if they did — it'd suck," Brockawitz said. "Nostalgia's one thing, but no way is some weed grown back in the 70's as good as Ambrosia, Acapulco Gold or Sweet Susie."

Coulter was drumming his fingers on his desk.

"I want to know everything there is to know about this Baby Bear's Bed company. Who is it? Where have they been growing weed? Who are they affiliated with? What kind of license do they have — medicinal or recreational? Who issued it? Do they have a patent?"

"Maybe they don't have either a patent or a license," Clifford said. "Maybe they're just 'in the wind.' They could be anywhere."

"Find them," Coulter said. "If it's good weed, I want it."

He clicked 'leave meeting,' watched the faces of Moe, Curly and Larry freeze in mid-expression before he flipped off the screen.

Righteous Weed. That struck a chord with Coulter — would make a similar connection to a whole generation of other stoners, too. It really had been the first weed Damien Coulter had ever smoked. Might be he'd stumbled upon the Holy Grail. Might be.

Chapter Twenty-One

It was evening. Sherry Lynn imagined she could hear the sound of the tractor out in a field, getting louder and louder and louder, then softer and softer and softer after it turned at the end of the row and went the other way. Like somebody was cutting wheat. It wasn't real, though. She knew there was no wheat growing at Land's End, or any other crop for that matter. Her son Drew raised thorough-bred horses.

Drew. That's who the young man was who'd told her she had pulled up all the tomato plants. Her own son, Drew. She hadn't, of course. Why would she uproot tomato plants? She loved tomatoes.

She could still hear the tractor, though. She knew it wasn't real, but she could still hear it. Wasn't that an odd thing. The auditory image had been burned into her brain during the years she was married to Tim Brand and lived on his farm on Crocker Pike, raising his three rowdy sons. They hadn't had much during those years. Lived in an old frame house on his family farm, with Tim growing corn, tobacco and breeding black angus cattle. It had been a far cry from the life she'd lived in the beautiful mansion with the roaring lions out front — that had surveillance cameras in their mouths, but nobody knew that part. The other end of the spectrum. Riches to rags, they'd call it.

Even though she sat with the air conditioner blowing cold air right into her face, she still felt hot. Flushed hot. She'd got Drew to install it in her bedroom because the central air conditioning didn't proper cool the top of the house. The way the heat rose in late August — one frying-pan day following another — she hadn't been able to sleep at night, couldn't seem to get cool enough.

Sherry Lynn couldn't cool off now, either, but it wasn't about August heat or central air conditioning. She was hot on the *inside* now.

She hadn't turned on the light in the room, just sat there in the shadows with the cold wind in her flushed face, feeling the chill of her wet clothes stick to her skin as the sweat slowly evaporated.

Growing weed.

Righteous Weed.

Those two words touched so many hot buttons within Sherry Lynn that she felt like she was being electrocuted. Like she was being shocked all over, lying on a wire mattress some psychopath had attached wires to so he could use it to torture his victims.

The words had pulled out the stops, collapsed a dam she didn't even know was there until it wasn't anymore. All the pain and misery had come flooding down the hillside and covered her up, got up to her chin, was about to drown her.

Awful images. Nightmare images.

They were like still photographs, illuminated by those flashbulbs you used to buy for small cameras, the little square ones that produced a brief light so bright you couldn't see afterwards.

Click-click.

Walking back into her mansion, empty, after she had been released from jail. *Jail!* She walked into the living room where there'd been a birthday party in progress until the FBI showed up. She'd been just about to introduce the clown to the crowd of children when she heard the doorbell ring.

And the doorbell had sounded sinister. It had! Even then, when she had no idea the horror that awaited her … even then the bell sounded menacing and she hadn't wanted to answer it. But she had. And they'd hauled her away in a state police cruiser while Drew and the other little kids stood wide-eyed on the porch watching.

The house was quiet by the time she got back. All the mess was gone — no presents or gift-wrapping, no decorations, no cake or melting ice cream. Somebody had cleaned it all up. She didn't know who. The only sound she could hear was the gentle clop of her footsteps and the sound of someone sobbing softly. It was her crying, but she didn't know that at the time.

The night in *jail,* though she was only locked up for eight or nine hours, had permanently changed Sherry Lynn Hannacker. She would never be the same again. It broke something. She'd felt it snap. It was like the rubber band inside a doll, stretched tight to hold the pieces of the doll in place, had broken, so the arms and legs just dangled. That was Sherry Lynn. All her pieces parts just dangled.

She couldn't look at anybody for months, didn't make eye contact for what felt like a year, slinked around, avoided everybody — except, Jessie, of course. Oh yeah, Jessie'd been there alright. Telling Sherry Lynn to be strong, that Drew needed her, that everything would be alright, that they'd get through this and go on with their lives.

Good ole Jessie. Yes sir-ee, right there whenever Sherry Lynn needed her. And in truth, Sherry Lynn might not have made it if she hadn't had Jessie to lean on. That's what made it so horrible, so awful, so unthinkable when she finally found out years later. *Years!* Jessie, the BFF she'd bonded with on that long drive home from Texas after the guard unit shipped out … Jessie had been sleeping with Sherry Lynn's husband the whole time, sneaking around behind her back.

Jessie claimed it'd just been one time. Right, one time. Who believed a tale like that? Sherry'd gotten pregnant with Drew after only one time, but that was different. Jessie and Riley … she was certain they'd been sleeping together for years. And poor Sherry Lynn never suspected a thing. Poor stupid Sherry Lynn believed Jessie was her friend and all the while Jessie's little girl … was Riley's daughter.

Ruth. Jessie's daughter Ruth. Somehow that witch had tricked poor Willa into some awful scheme to grow marijuana again. To grow Righteous Weed.

Drew had told Sherry Lynn before Christmas that Jessie was dead, that she'd been killed in that tornado that hit western Kentucky. Now, Sherry Lynn knew that'd been a lie. Jessie wasn't dead. Jessie was very much alive, was using her witch daughter to manipulate Willa. Sherry Lynn didn't know exactly how the whole thing was supposed to play out, but she'd find out. She'd uncover the whole plot, and then she'd show them what it felt like to be betrayed.

Sherry Lynn would put a stop to their grand plans if it was the last thing she ever did.

Chapter Twenty-Two

Damien Coulter looked down at the report on his desk, his eyes flicking over the words Righteous Weed highlighted in bright yellow, and thought about how he'd stolen Joe Ferguson's pencil box the day he smoked his first joint and the pencil box had had a yellow highlighter in it and that's what got Damien caught.

Sister Marie Celeste had gotten her nose way too out of joint about the theft — like Damien'd done it because he gave a rip about the stupid pencils and yellow highlighter. He'd lifted it accidentally, thought it was Joe's lunchbox and not some dumb pencil box, and Damien was suffering from his first and arguably his most severe case of the munchies he'd ever had in his life.

Damien'd got caught because he'd used the highlighter. A pencil is a pencil, he could pass the rest of the contents of the box off as his own, but not the highlighter. He'd used it, the prissy old nun had seen it, demanded to search his locker and bada boom, bada bing, found the roach he'd saved from that first memorable joint in the box among the pencils. Damien Coulter had been summarily thrown out of St. Gregory's school for boys. He was only twelve years old, had no idea what he was doing when the older boys shared their weed with him, thought he was smoking a cigarette — just one you rolled yourself like his uncle Phil did.

He'd inhaled and …

Yeah, he supposed he'd romanticized the experience, like every other stoner — that "first high" — can you hear the bands playing? But he really didn't think he was. Some people had to smoke two or three joints before they ever "felt anything." He did not number among those unfortunate souls. He took one toke off the fat "cigarette" sixteen-year-old Beto O'Malley handed to him, and he felt a sensation he'd been totally unprepared for.

He zoned.

He floated.

He felt at peace with the world, a partner of the universe … and, oh, by the way, so hungry he swallowed the contents of his own lunch sack in two bites, and then spotted what he thought was Joe Ferguson's lunch box left unattended.

It was Damien's first scrape with the authorities, so his parents dutifully hauled him across Atlanta to some other Catholic school. He hadn't been there a week before he found the pusher. He bought. He smoked. And he was disappointed.

At the time, he didn't know there were strains of weed, that they had names and certain characteristics and you could shop around until you found something you liked. He shopped, but never found the Nirvana of that first experience.

Had that lone joint been "Righteous Weed?" Maybe. The timeframe was right. It was the undisputed standard of excellence for nationally grown weed at that time, would have been billed "the best weed there is," and that's what he'd been told he was smoking.

Damien had been searching for that weed, for that experience, ever since, as had a whole lot of other weed smokers. In that pursuit, he had gone from consumer to provider before he was out of middle school — hawking weed in exchange for contributions to his own personal supply. His family moved out of the city in the vain hope that a rural, less metropolitan setting would change the trajectory of their only son's life back onto the straight and narrow. He quickly became "the man" in high school, when he and his buddies traveled to Atlanta to purchase weed to take back out into the hinterlands and to sell to the locals. Their supplier in Atlanta, a man he knew only as Bosco, took a liking to Damien and took the boy with him to New York City, where Bosco sold his own Georgia-grown weed and purchased different strains for distribution.

Bosco's supplier in New York was a black man who'd lost his leg in some famous battle in Vietnam. The man's name was Ace, and from him Damien learned firsthand about the Cornbread Mafia ... and idolized them. They were folk heroes. He wanted to *be* them. After he grew his first crop, using seeds he'd gotten out of the bottom of a baggie of weed to plant five scrawny marijuana plants between the rows of a neighbor's corn crop, he branched out into bigger fields. Damien Coulter was on his way.

He grew weed and sold it, and although smoking it never did get him to that place he'd first encountered, he managed to put together a weed operation that provided marijuana to dealers all over Georgia before his twenty-fifth birthday. Then all over the southeastern United States. A couple of near-misses — running through a weed field with a DEA chopper hanging in the sky overhead —

convinced him to clean up his act. When Ronald Reagan's War on Drugs slammed American growers into federal prisons on mandatory twenty-year sentences, Damien moved his operation offshore, found a way to launder his money, invested in legitimate businesses. He got a college education, met the right people, formed the right alliances, went up the ladder to success. Seven years ago, he'd founded a cannabis company called CoulterCulture Cannbis, Inc., grew acres of licensed weed in five states, harvested it with machinery, and mass produced edibles for sale all over the county.

He'd long since given up his quest for the Holy Grail of marijuana, weed that would reproduce the experience he'd had with the joint that'd sent him scavenging for other kids' lunch boxes when he was twelve years old. Then he kept tripping over references to Righteous Weed and he wondered. Was it possible …?

Looking up from the report, he eyed Russell Brockawitz, who'd crawled out of a hole somewhere in the wilds of Oklahoma to chase down leads.

"So Baby Bear's Bed is a dummy corporation?"

"Kinda like one of those Russian stacking dolls. It's one shell corporation inside a bigger shell corporation inside … We do know that whoever is running it has spent more than thirty thousand dollars on advertising."

"That's a lot of money to invest in a charade."

"I don't know how much you know about the original Righteous Weed, but it was grown by a cartel called the Cornbread Mafia and they went down hard. The whole circus tent fell down around their heads more than thirty years ago, busted maybe a hundred workers in fields all over the country, hauled them off—"

"I know all about the Cornbread Mafia. What's your point?"

"Just that they all came from the same place, this little county called—"

"Callison County, Kentucky. I know. Tell me something I don't know."

"The fellow who took the biggest hit was Riley Hannacker, and he's still alive, got out after twenty years in federal prison and still lives in Callison County, Kentucky."

That was interesting.

"He's growing weed there?"

"Not that anybody knows about."

Damien had a thought.

"You don't suppose he still has … seed …?"

"That he's been sitting on for four decades? Not likely. But if he developed the original Righteous Weed strain, maybe he's managed to come up with some kind of knock-off. They'd have to believe what they've got is close enough to pass or they wouldn't dare hype it as the real thing."

That made sense.

"If that's the case, just some old guy and a couple of his cronies," Brockawitz continued, "they're operating on a shoestring."

"And you're thinking maybe they'd be willing to sell?"

"To somebody who could produce it on a scale that'd make ten times what they could make — why not?"

Right. Why not? Unless money wasn't their only motivation.

"And if they're disinclined to sell?"

Coulter smiled. "We will make them an offer they can't refuse."

Chapter Twenty-Three

Willa had been right. No big surprise there. Willa Hannacker didn't miss much. She'd said from the git-go that there was way more illegal weed on the market in 2022 than there was legal weed. She had certainly nailed that one. Ruth had been on the road for almost three months now, hawking a product that didn't yet exist — with a wink and a nod — to dispensaries all over eleven states. Ruth'd learned quick that there was "over-the-table" weed — sold through licensed dispensaries that had purchased it from growers who'd been licensed to grow it. It'd been approved, stamped and taxed. Then there was "under the table" weed that a reputable, licensed dispensary was not allowed to sell, illegal weed grown by who-knew-who, who-knew-where, no license, no taxes, no fees.

Why would a reputable establishment buy illegal weed? Well, duh. For the same reasons nightclubs and restaurant owners bought bootleg hootch. Great product, great price. The essence of American capitalism at work. Illegal weed in today's marketplace was better weed — which stuck in the craws of the big operations ... that were mostly run by small growers who'd branched out, and every small grower on the planet was hooked on the pursuit of the Holy Grail — the mystical, magical marijuana strain that was the best in the world. The research and development departments in Big Canna Land were peopled by — as Willa put it — a bunch of lost ducks in high weeds honking out one product after another when not a one of them had any real idea where the pond was. Those guys were "scientists," botanists and agri-business professionals, who could actually genetically clone one plant from another one. But it was the little growers out there in the hinterlands, splicing one strain of weed to another, who were on the cutting edge — "the final frontier." The farmers who'd grow a hundred plants and cut down ninety-nine of them — always looking for the best, the best, the *best.* Those guys were where the really good weed was coming from. Some things never changed.

The advertising Baby Bear's Bed had purchased had created a buzz in the cannabis community that was as deafening as the cry of those cicadas that came out of the ground every seven years. Every dispensary Ruth talked to was "interested." Their interest ranged along a scale from mildly curious to stoners with the munchies staring at a piece of chocolate cake.

Ruth smiled at the big man with the eyepatch. He was the right age, build and demeanor — he could have lost that eye to an IED in Afghanistan like that congressman from Texas. He also could have put it out with a sharp stick when he was in second grade.

The man stuck out his hand to shake Ruth's. "Look forward to taking a look at your product ... *ma'am.*" Ruth always introduced herself as "a representative of Baby Bear's Bed," and didn't offer a name. She would have told him who she was if he'd asked, but he didn't. None of them did. The quasi-anonymity of namelessness was part of the wink-and-nod game you played when you were hawking unlicensed weed — weed that came in the back door, marijuana everybody involved acknowledged was lightyears better than what came in the front.

As the man crossed back through the field of broad, waist-high marijuana plants that looked like little Christmas trees, toward his office building, Ruth set out toward her rental car in the parking lot, making notations on the bottom line of a tally sheet before she returned it to the folder in her backpack. Willa rolled her eyes at that, couldn't understand why Ruth didn't record all her information in an iPad. It wasn't that Ruth was old-school like her father, who made no secret of the fact that he believed anybody who could operate any device more complicated than a flip-phone was a witch and should be burned at the stake. Ruth used pen and paper because she had first organized her businesses — Ruth's Stuff and Has-Beens — by spreading papers all over the floor of her tiny apartment in Chicago, spreadsheets and product inventories and profit-and-loss statements. She didn't know why it was, but she seemed able to keep a multitude of divergent facts and pieces of information "top of mind" if she could envision them on sheets of paper.

Top of mind. If there was a top of mind, there was also a bottom. And that's the spot currently populated by most everything else in Ruth Hannacker's life besides weed. A pang of guilt made its way through the exhausted synapses in her brain as she got into the car behind the wheel. She'd received — and ignored — half a dozen texts from her attorneys in the past couple of days and the lawyers were not trying to reach her in regard to the button-button-who's-got-the-button shell game of corporations they'd created to obscure the identity of the owners of Baby Bear's Bed. They were concerned about Ruth's other businesses, the ones that'd meant the world to her just a couple of months ago, the ones she had spent fifteen years growing into thriving concerns.

The remaining handful of Ruth's Stuff stores was on the ropes. Has-Beens was in equally dire straits. She understood somewhere in her tired mind that if she tried, really *tried*, knuckled down and worked her butt off, she could salvage something from the two corporations about to go belly-up. It would take a huge amount of effort to right the ships, but it was possible.

There had been a time when she thought all was lost, but the market had rebounded enough in her little niche to make an opening she could squeeze through. But time was running out. Time. That was the thing, the commodity that couldn't be "scaled." The number of hours in the day remained the same, and the amount of activity you could jam into those hours was finite as well. Bottom line, she could not devote her every waking hour to making a go of Baby Bear's Bed and devote an equal amount of time to resurrecting her other businesses. Not without being twins. She would have to decide between them, but even that decision was rapidly sliding out of her reach. It wouldn't be long, a month or two maybe, before the life support systems for her two ailing corporations would fail. The employees she'd told to "handle it" could only handle so much. She had built the businesses — on the power of her personality and the strength of her will. Without Ruth to fuel the effort, it would ultimately be a lost cause.

Did that matter? Given the future out there awaiting the launch of Righteous Weed into the cannabis market, what difference did that make? She would be in charge of getting Baby Bear's Bed up and running, would be at the helm of an entity operating in the rarified air of "multi-million-dollar finance." If she chose to, she could infuse some of that capital into patching up the holes in her other business ventures, could run the whole thing.

That sounded … exhausting.

She glanced up into the rearview mirror of the car she'd driven over half the county roads in Oklahoma. Bad move. The face that stared back at her looked ancient. Okay, not ancient. But old, definitely old. Old*er* than she'd been in the spring when she'd first crawled down between the boulders at the edge of a new-growth forest and found the treasure of the Tree House. She'd lost weight. But Willa'd lost more, she thought with a sense of triumph that made no sense at all. Willa had been running on empty ever since her boyfriend made it clear he didn't want to be involved with a criminal.

Willa'd lost Isaiah.

And Ruth had lost … what? Well, her businesses. But look what she'd gained. Look what both of them had *gained*. The sacrifice had been worth it. It had, hadn't it?

She put the key in the ignition and quickly plugged in her phone, which was low on juice. It rang while she had it in her hand. It was Papa.

"How'd it go with Thurston?"

Thurston and Sons, Cannabis Distributors. Ruth had just met the owner's son — the guy who lost an eye to an IED or a sharp stick, one or the other.

"On the 'try it and see' list."

"That's getting to be a pretty long list, isn't it?"

"It is. I'll show you a spreadsheet—"

"A list is fine."

"A list it is, then. What's up?"

"You be back home by tomorrow?"

"Unless the flight's cancelled because some jackass gets

into a fight with a flight attendant over having to wear a face mask."

Though only a couple of airlines were still holdouts, that'd happened several times in the spring, and Ruth had gotten stuck overnight once in Grand Rapids, Michigan. Pointless. Little pieces of paper over everybody's faces — like that was *ever* anything but a total joke. Eventually the idiots who'd said the masks worked changed course and said they'd been against masks all along. Surely, Southwest Airlines had thrown in the towel by now and she could fly back to Louisville in peace.

"Maybe you'll get here in time to meet Damien Coulter. He's stopping by to see me."

"*The* Damien Coulter, CEO of CoulterCulture?"

"I don't s'pose there's but one Damien Coulter."

"You buried the lede, Papa."

"Huh?"

"That means you should have told me that in the beginning."

"Told you what?"

"About Coulter."

"I just did."

"Never mind."

"Wouldn't say what he wanted, but I figure he ain't trying to sign me up for Amway."

"Amway? What's—"

"Never mind."

"It's a big deal when the mountain decides to come to Mohammed. Appears we've made it into the dialogue around corporate boardrooms."

"Guess we'll find out tomorrow what they're saying."

Chapter Twenty-Four

Riley sat reading the *Callison County Tribune*'s Tuesday issue
— where the lead story concerned two local teenagers
who'd died from overdosing on fentanyl. Jessie had taught
both of them in third grade! The story said the sheriff had
traced the source of the drug to a gang of illegal immi-
grants who'd waded across the Rio Grande River just a
week before. How could—?

He heard a knock on the front door and was grateful to
be interrupted. That was good, the knock part. There was
a doorbell set in the wood of the doorframe, put there
when Jessie'd renovated the house for Willie Ray, who'd
liked listening to the tinkling sound it made. When Riley
got out of prison and moved in here with Jessie, he'd kinda
used the chime as a bellwether. If a visitor rang the bell,
they were the kind of person who followed rules. If they
ignored the bell and just knocked, they were everybody
else.

Riley opened the door to find a tall, lean man with
sharp features standing on the other side. His hair was the
color of a ten-penny nail and he wore it short — what the

kids called "high and tight." That usually meant one of two things — the guy was former military, or he wanted you to think he was.

"Are you Riley Hannacker? I'm Damien Coulter."

Riley stepped aside and shoved the door open, held out his hand and the man shook it. Just like Riley's father'd taught him, the way Riley'd taught Drew. When you shake a man's hand you give him a firm grip, look him in the eye, once up, once down — anybody wants to pump up and down like they're trying to draw water out of a well ain't to be trusted.

"Come on into the kitchen. I can't operate one of them coffee machine things but I know my way around a plain old coffee pot if you'd like a cup."

The man followed Riley into the kitchen, looking around.

"This the place they shot up — that Colombian drug cartel?"

Riley about dropped his coffee cup. He found his voice as he gestured for the man to sit down at the table.

"Not many folks left who know that old tale. Took a week and a couple of jars of plastic wood to plug up all the holes." He gestured to a sugar bowl on the table. "I got cream, too, if—"

"Black's fine, thanks."

The man sat down in front of the cup of coffee Riley'd set on the table.

"I heard the story from Ace."

The name got Riley's attention. Clearly, that was Coulter's intent.

"He and I go way back. Not as far back as the two of you, of course, but ... I began doing business with him in 1990 or '91, I think. I was just a kid, working in a weed field in Georgia. Sometimes the boss'd take me with him to

New York City to sell it to Ace." He smiled. "That man had all kinds of stories about the exploits of the Cornbread Mafia and it didn't take a whole lot of prodding to get him going. He said he'd managed to remain invisible when the feds made the big bust — 'it's easy to hide in the dark if you's black — just gotta remember to keep your eyes closed.'"

Riley chuckled.

Ace absolutely woulda said that — *testing*, his guard up, watching the white guy's face, eyes mostly, that's where it usually showed up. Never took Ace more'n five seconds to take a man's measure. Riley would dearly like to know what Ace's assessment of Damien Coulter had been. But Ace was gone. Cancer. Hearing Ace's words was like bringing his friend briefly to life, though, right there in his kitchen. It was bittersweet.

"He told me all about the attack of the Colombians, said you named your strain Righteous Weed because he told you when he lit your first joint back in Vietnam that the weed he sold was 'righteous.'"

Smooth.

The man had taken hold of the conversation as soon as he walked in the door and was now driving it down the interstate where he wanted it to go — exit ramp "Righteous Weed" one mile ahead, on the right.

Damien Coulter was charming and likable. Even if his aw-shucks routine was a little rusty, it was clear he probably really had been a Georgia cracker once. Years ago. Years and jobs and careers and millions of dollars ago.

So why'd he decide he needed to haul out the persona, blow the dust off it and parade it in front of Riley? Riley was pretty sure Mr. Coulter didn't go to the office every day dressed as he was dressed right now — chambray shirt and a pair of jeans. Wasn't that it looked like some kind of costume, like it wasn't real. The jeans weren't stylishly frayed and the shirt had a cuff button missing. They were his clothes alright; Riley figured he actually wore them in real life and real time. But that wasn't the question. Why had he worn them here today to talk to Riley? Dress Casual Thursday at CoulterCulture, the cannabis company Ruth said was one of the largest in the country?

Aw, maybe Riley was overthinking it. Assigning meaning and calculation where there was none. It was just that he couldn't shake his initial gut reaction to the man. He had instantly disliked him. And didn't trust him. No reason, just didn't. Like an old dog who growls at a stranger, and you don't know what it is about the stranger that the dog can see or smell or sense that you can't, but most times old dogs was right.

Riley decided not to wait for the exit ramp.

"You're here because you want to talk about Righteous Weed, least that's what I figure."

"I do."

"I've heard about the magazine ads; my kids have seen the social media posts. 'Pears somebody somewhere is growing marijuana they're claiming is Righteous Weed — and you think it's me. A reasonable assumption, I guess. I probably woulda thought the same, but then we'd both be wrong. I haven't been in the weed business in four decades, haven't grown a crop since 1979. I coulda told you that on the phone if you'd told me what you wanted. Saved you coming all this way for nothing."

Coulter didn't say anything for a beat.

"Oh, I don't think the trip's wasted. I've wanted to come to Callison County for years. I'm sure you guys know you were something like folk heroes to a whole generation of kids who wanted—"

"To spend twenty years locked in a cage with a metal

toilet attached to the wall that flushes every hour whether you take a dump in it or not?"

Riley judged by how quickly Coulter recovered that he'd had a lot of practice balancing on a spinning log in the river, not getting knocked off by the other guy on the log next to you. His face closed up some, though, the edges of the grin melted downward.

"Lotta people lost a lotta years of living for nothing more than growing a crop. I'm sorry you were one of them." A beat. "But times have changed. The Cultivation Division of CoulterCulture currently farms four ten-acre plots in Oklahoma, along with smaller farms and greenhouses in Colorado, Florida and Nevada. I don't know if you're aware of the size of the cannabis industry in the U.S. — it was worth sixteen billion last year and twenty billion worldwide. Even without further legalization, the medical and recreational cannabis industry is expected to grow at an annual rate of more than thirty percent between now and 2024."

"Good to hear the weed business is looking up, but I don't see how that has anything to do with me."

"A company called Baby Bear's Bed is advertising it will have Righteous Weed for sale this fall."

"Baby Bear's Bed?" Riley pretended to figure it out. "Oh, because it's just right."

Coulter wasn't fooled.

"Yeah, just right. They're claiming it's the *original* Righteous Weed. Since you're the man who raised the original, I'm wondering … do you have any idea why somebody would make a claim like that?"

"No idea whatsoever."

"Could it possibly be true?"

"That it's the original Righteous Weed?" He shrugged. "I s'pose anything's possible."

The man sat back in his chair, considering.

"Indulge me, if you will, Mr. Hannacker. Just for the sake of discussion, let's say you are growing Righteous Weed. That'd mean you've been sitting on Righteous Weed seeds for four decades. Why *now*?"

Riley looked at him, said nothing.

"Decided to make it a family business, did you — a new generation of Hannackers and Taggarts and Monaghans want you to pass the baton?"

Still, Riley didn't speak.

"If you are growing it, you don't have a license. I've checked."

"That'd make it illegal, then, wouldn't it? Why would I get mixed up in something like illegal weed again after all these years?" He should have left it at that, but he didn't. "It is my understanding, though, that there's way more illegal weed out there on the market right now than legal. I'm told, and I could be wrong, of course, that the illegal weed's a better product than the legal."

"Baby Bear's Bed apparently thinks so. They're asking four thousand, maybe forty-five hundred dollars a pound for it. Was the *original* Righteous Weed worth that kind of money?"

"Every dime of it. Willie Ray's was the best strain of marijuana ever produced. Of course, that was back when … Richard Nixon was president and far's I know, ain't nobody raised any since."

Coulter leaned back in his chair. "At that price, you could just about grow enough in your garage to make a million dollars."

Riley shrugged.

Coulter leaned forward and put his elbows on the table.

"Let me paint a different scenario for you. Consider

the kind of money … *somebody* could make if they had the resources to grow more than a garage full. An acre'd be worth what … fifty, seventy-five million dollars. And as I understand it, the Cornbread Mafia used to grow weed in *five-acre* plots."

Riley shrugged. "My granddaughter says with some things, less is more."

"I beg to differ with your granddaughter — when you're talking about marijuana, *more* is more. Grow Righteous Weed in a licensed field and—"

"That'd be outdoors, industrial farming. Mow it down with some kind of machine and mash it into a "bio-mass" — I don't imagine you could get four thousand dollars a pound for green goo."

"No, but on that scale, the quantity—"

"*Quantity* … acres and acres of licensed fields of Righteous Weed?"

"You could make a fortune."

"*Somebody* could make a fortune. Not me. Remember, I ain't growing nothing." Again, he should have left it at that. But he didn't. "And even if I were, I wouldn't be interested in a deal like that."

"You can't not be interested until you hear what I'm offering."

"Yeah, actually, I can."

Coulter paused, took a breath, pivoted.

"I'm also prepared to purchase the seed outright, straight one-time purchase with a contract so the owner of the weed collects a percentage of every pound—"

"You need to find the owner of that weed and make him that offer, Mr. Coulter, see what he says. But me … I ain't growing nothin' so I ain't got no seed to sell."

"You're passing up an opportunity—"

Riley got to his feet.

"We just talking in circles, Mr. Coulter, not getting nowhere. You're barking up the wrong tree." For the third time that morning, he should have left it at that. But he didn't. "Now, if I happen to stumble upon whoever *is* growing that weed, I'll tell him to give you a call."

There was just a flash, and afterward Riley wasn't even certain he'd seen it. Coulda been a trick of the light. But for just a moment, Riley saw something in the man's eyes. Something predatory, wild and dangerous. His expression never changed, and that was telling, too. He wasn't disappointed, didn't try to convince, just rolled over and gave up without a fight.

How come?

You go to all kinda trouble, get all dressed down in normal-people clothes, come all this way to make an offer, the guy says no, and you pick up your marbles and go home? No pushback at all? No dickering/persuading/counter-offer? That was all wrong. The Damien Coulters of this world got to be in charge of their own little corners of it by getting what they wanted. Every time.

So why didn't he … unless he figured out it was a lost cause, and backed up to punt. Already had in mind some kind of Plan B, some *other* way to get Righteous Weed without *buying* it.

And there wasn't but one other way Riley could think of to do that.

Chapter Twenty-Five

It appeared in the air in front of Sherry Lynn, floating there, outlined with a golden haze like the sun coming up over the top of a knob on a frosty fall morning, or a foggy spring one.

She'd heard the term Fabergé egg her whole life but until she saw that first one in the home decor department in Macy's when she was picking out the furnishings for their new house, she didn't have any idea how lovely one could be.

It was the size and shape of an egg, of course, sitting up on its end in a little gold stand. This one was called "Strawberry Celebration," and the outside of the metal egg was covered in rubies and garnets, giving it the pitted look of a strawberry. A gold stem with green emerald leaves protruded from the top. And when you opened it up at the center hinge, you found inside a delicate tiny strawberry shortcake that took her breath away — made of rubies and dozens of tiny diamonds.

Not a real Fabergé egg, of course. Those things cost millions. But she'd determined the day she saw this one that someday, some day, she would own one that was authentic.

Sherry Lynn started to reach for it, but didn't, just stared in fascination at how unutterably beautiful it was.

Even this knockoff, made with real gold, real silver, real diamonds, emeralds and garnets and rubies, cost almost twenty thousand dollars. She heard the voice of the New York decorator she'd hired to help her furnish her Callison County mansion with the very best of everything — then fired her because she had dared to suggest that the things Sherry Lynn wanted were … gauche. No, not the things, the number of them.

One Fabergé egg was elegant, half a dozen was over the top. Less was more, the woman'd said.

No, sorry Madeline, more is more!

Her name was Madeline, just Madeline, a single name. Sherry Lynn was sure the lack of a surname added twenty percent to the price of every item she sold and an additional thirty to the cost of getting her professional opinion.

"Be sure to balance your lighting," said a voice from the other room. Madeline. But Sherry Lynn didn't turn her attention away from the egg floating daintily in the air in front of her. "Go large-scale with art — one large canvas to dominate the wall, not three little ones." And one large statue, well, okay, two, the two lions, to dominate the entrance to the house. Light candles at the end of a stressful day and always remember fresh flowers have power.

Sherry Lynn reached out her hand to the egg … and watched her fingers pass through it as if it were a mirage. It still hung there in the air, and suddenly the whole room was full of beautiful things, the vase with the fluted top like a peacock's feathers, the Waterford Crystal, each individual piece … all floating there, and then they blinked out of existence one at a time, leaving a little soap-bubble sparkle in the air.

Gone.

Gone. *Gone.*

Sherry Lynn had had all the beautiful things she had ever wanted … and then they were gone.

She closed her eyes and opened them again slowly. The beautiful things and the sparkles they'd left behind when they vanished were gone. The den in Drew's renovated carriage house at Land's End came into crisp focus, and instead of Madeline's voice in the other room, she heard her granddaughter Lissy's, clearly upset.

"… don't know who *else* Luna and Chase might have told that Willa's growing *Righteous Weed* at Land's End …"

Drew's voice. Strong, unflappable, loyal Drew.

"Don't worry about it, Lissy. They'll forget the words in a few days."

"I could talk to them about what 'righteous' means, you know, tell Luna it means 'holy,' so it's really 'holy weed,' and that's what she and Chase should call it—"

"I think you're better off to ignore the whole thing. Make a big deal out of it and they're more likely to remember. If they do say it — who'll know what they mean? Or care?"

Sherry Lynn knew, though.

Sherry Lynn cared.

Righteous Weed had paid for all the pretty things. She looked around in the room, pleading with the shadows to give up their images again, but nothing appeared.

All Sherry Lynn's beautiful things, anything she wanted, that's what Riley'd told her — she could have *anything* she wanted. Righteous Weed had paid the freight on her home and swimming pools and sports cars. The weed Riley and the others grew paid for everything. But who knew it could turn on them? Who knew that at any moment it could turn on them and gobble them up?

For a moment the world around her grew dim and she could hear voices from that place, the dark place where words echoed in hollow tones.

"Sherry Lynn Hannacker, you are under arrest."

Under arrest.

The bars and the banging of the cell doors and that woman down the hall who keeps screaming and screaming and …

"Mom, are you okay?"

No one was there and then Drew was there with Andrea. Nobody, then Drew and Andrea. They just appeared — like the pretty things — but they're not floating in the air in golden light. They're standing next to her and Drew has that look of concern stapled between his eyebrows. That look of concern, the one that says, 'you're not making sense,' when the truth was that Sherry Lynn was making perfect sense. If they couldn't understand her, they were the ones with the problem.

Was she okay? they wanted to know. Of course she wasn't okay. All the pretty things were gone, the egg — more, she'd gotten half a dozen — and the peacock vase and the sweet little Stingray that …

"Mom?"

"What," she barked testily. "How could I be okay when it was there and now it's all gone again? But I know what happened to it. I know *who* took it. Don't think for a minute I was fooled. She took all my pretty things, wanted them and took them and left me with nothing. But I won't let her do it again. No sir! Fool me once, shame on you, fool me twice, shame on me."

"What are you talking about?" Drew asked.

She couldn't tell him, of course. He was her only son, the precious little boy to whom she'd devoted her whole life, but she couldn't tell him that she wasn't going to let it slide. They took all her pretty things and they had to pay.

She ground her teeth until her jaw began to ache.

If I can't have pretty things, nobody can.

Sherry Lynn brushed past her son and out the door of the room into a long hallway that led … somewhere. She wasn't sure where. Stairs maybe. But as she walked, she began to lose a grip on where she was going, as she had lost a grip on why she was so determined to go there.

Righteous Weed.

It had something to do with Righteous Weed.

She just wasn't sure what. But she'd remember. It would come back to her. It always did.

Chapter Twenty-Six

Damien Coulter stepped off the porch after Riley Hannacker had summarily given him his walking papers and shown him to the door, and started toward the rented Lexus he'd picked up when he flew into Louisville International Airport on the company jet last night. He'd spent a few moments examining the porch when he'd arrived, before he knocked. It was foolish, of course, to think he might spot one of the bullet holes now — he knew that. It'd been repaired almost *fifty years ago*, probably had been painted a dozen times since then. The old house was in remarkably good shape — it was clear somebody'd spent a small fortune to maintain it mostly "just like it was." But Ace's description of that long-ago shootout had so fascinated Damien when he was still too young to order a beer in a bar that coming here felt a little like going to the Alamo. There was a flowering dogwood tree in the front yard now, not the sycamore tree where Riley'd crouched in the limbs waiting for the Colombians to stop shooting. Azalea bushes had replaced the original oleander bushes around the bathtub Mary that still sat in the yard, their brilliant hot-pink flowers —

He paused halfway down the sidewalk that hadn't existed half a century ago and stood for a moment looking at the grotto — the Virgin Mary statue made into a shrine sunk inside half an old cast-iron bathtub. He'd seen others like it as he drove through the county.

Turning off the sidewalk, he walked to the shrine for a better look, and a broad grin spread across his face. He could see a single round hole on the top right edge of the bathtub, could have been a bullet hole. Or not. Well, he chose to believe it was, and that it was the result of a stray bullet fired that night. He reached out and plucked one of the pink blossoms, put it to his nose and inhaled the fragrant aroma, continued to his car and drove away.

His cell rang as he was turning out of the driveway; he looked at the caller — Russell Brockawitz — and sent it to voicemail. Brockawitz was calling to find out how the meeting had gone and Damien wanted to get his own mind around it before he started getting input from others.

So what did Damien Coulter think?

He thought Riley Hannacker was one tough old bird! He had to be seventy-five — no, not quite that, seventy-one or two. He looked every day of it — with deep sun wrinkles and pure white hair, but he hadn't lost a single step. He was as quick as a rattlesnake. Before Damien took his first sip of coffee, he had figured out his was a lost cause.

Oh, Hannacker was growing it alright. Of course he was. Damien knew that and the old guy knew Damien knew. But the man wouldn't have admitted it if Damien had pulled out a cashier's check for ten million dollars and plopped it on the table.

Damien didn't think it was about the money for

Hannacker. Maybe it had been once, a long time ago, but things were different now. Times were different. Hannacker was different. Maybe he'd resurrected Righteous Weed because it was "the family business." He was passing the torch. As such, he wouldn't have the slightest interest in selling off that business to corporate America — didn't matter what the price tag was.

But that analysis didn't answer the central question of why now? Or the central practical question of *how* now?

What was the spark that'd lit the old man's fire? If it really was the real deal, the only possible explanation was that Riley Hannacker had been sitting on Righteous Weed seeds for four decades ... and then one morning he gets out of bed, stretches, yawns and while he's brushing his teeth he decides to start growing it again and make millions of dollars?

Maybe it had something to do with his wife's death right before Christmas. She was killed by a tornado in December ... and then he decided to grow forty-five-year-old Righteous Weed seeds in March. Was there a connection? If that was it, there was a big piece missing. Maybe it was about his kids' finances. He'd checked them out. Ruth Hannacker was hanging onto her corporations — Ruth's Stuff and Has-Beens — by her fingernails. They'd been hammered hard by the pandemic. She wasn't totally underwater yet but the ship was definitely sinking. His son, Drew, owned a horse farm that was on the ropes. The whole thoroughbred industry was. Might sink, might swim, too soon to tell. But the thing was — you could probably have made the same financial analysis of the situation six months, maybe even a year ago and Papa hadn't come running to the rescue with a bag of seeds and a determination to plant a beanstalk then. Why *now*?

It would reeeeally help to understand the motivation

here, but Damien was beginning to suspect he was destined to come up snake eyes on that one. Which left Central Question number two. If not why, then *how*? Baby Bear's Bed, Inc., was offering Righteous Weed for sale, deliverable before Christmas. Hannacker was growing that crop right now … *somewhere*. Where?

And after this morning's meeting, it was clear that was the only question that really mattered. If he could have figured out the motivation, Damien could have tailored an offer to fit. Without knowing Hannacker's why, he was just throwing shit up on the wall to see if anything would stick.

Rounding a corner, Damien almost rear-ended a pickup truck puttering along behind a hay wagon making its wobbly way down the center of the highway behind a tractor. He checked his instinctive reaction to honk. What for? There wasn't enough room to pass the hay wagon and clearly the tractor pulling it was going as fast as it could. He and the pickup truck were stuck behind it until it turned off the road. Damien glanced at the bumper stickers on the pickup, a shiny new Ford F-250. One was the simple Christian "fish" shape. One said "I bleed University of Kentucky blue." The third featured the face of Joe Biden, looking confused, above the caption: "The five scariest words in the English language — Senile. Dementia. Only. Gets. *Worse*."

He chuckled. Yep, this was definitely MAGA country. Damien shook his head, then reminded himself that previous generations of these people had concealed a multi-million-dollar marijuana-growing cartel, so respect for authority and the rule of law had not historically been a value here.

The Cornbread Mafia had once raised acres of weed in Callison County, but outdoor weed wasn't what Baby Bear's Bed was offering for sale. Boutique marijuana, harvested and trimmed by hand. Where were they growing *that?*

In Kentucky illegally?

Out of state legally — on some plot of land, using somebody else's license?

Indoor/greenhouse or even hydroponics?

That was what Damien Coulter had to find out. Because at some time in the past half hour, his mind had weighed the evidence, compared his options and come up with a plan of action.

His conclusions:

First, Damien didn't know what Riley Hannacker's motivation was but he was convinced he knew what it wasn't — money. So Damien's typical fallback — retreat, gather more information, probe for a weak spot, offer a sweeter deal — was pointless.

Two, if Damien Coulter couldn't *buy* Righteous Weed, the only way he could get his hands on it was to steal it. He would have to find out where they were growing it, sneak in and steal a couple of plants. He'd use cell culture techniques to make a synthetic embryo, a genetic duplicate of Righteous Weed. Then he'd grow a plant and *patent it.*

So Hannacker wins this year. He sells his famous weed. He makes a boatload of money. Actually, he'd be paving the way, proving the quality of the product, and amassing a horde of hungry buyers for next year.

Damien Coulter would be standing in the wings, ready next year to take it all. CoulterCulture would grow *acres* of Righteous Weed and send an army of lawyers after Hannacker when he competed.

The phone rang again and he took the call, but he cut Brockawitz off before he had a chance to say hello.

"I want to know where Riley Hannacker is growing Righteous Weed. I don't care how much it costs. I don't care who you have to bribe, whose arm you have to twist, who you have to intimidate. Dig into the Hannacker family's lives — look for bones in a closet. A disgruntled employee maybe." Fat chance, that. One reason the Cornbread Mafia had become a legend was their code of silence. Nobody ... a hundred or so busts and not one person had cut a deal with the feds. Well, that was then. This was now. "Look for somebody with an ax to grind against Hannacker. Somebody somewhere knows something. For the right price, they'll talk. Find. That. Weed."

Chapter Twenty-Seven

"I've decided what I want for my birthday next week," Sherry Lynn announced at breakfast.

Drew and Andrea exchanged a glance. Did they really think she was so stupid she didn't pick up on those looks? Well, let them think so. Sherry Lynn knew her birthday wasn't Friday. It was in January. But they didn't know she knew that ... oh, she'd figured the whole thing out as she lay in bed last night, visions of her "pretty things" blinking on and off in her room like Fourth of July sparklers.

"Birthday?" Drew said.

"Oh, don't act like you forgot. You never forget." Sherry Lynn acted like an idea had just struck her. "And don't pretend you don't know because you're really planning a surprise birthday party. No party!"

Drew smiled at her.

"Deal. No party."

Drew didn't look well, hadn't looked well for ... she couldn't remember how long. Stress, of course. Everybody was stressed. Lock the whole country up and throw away the key for a year and that's what you got. A year's worth of cabin fever. And since Sherry Lynn was "the target market" — meaning over the age of sixty-five — they'd socked her away in the house and wouldn't let her go anywhere, wouldn't let anybody come to visit either. She knew the pandemic had screwed with the finances of the whole planet, but she suspected people like Drew — whose professions were definitely non-essential — had been hurt maybe worse than most. Land's End had been doing well before COVID. But now … bleeding money to feed horses that never raced and brought home winnings, that never bred and dropped a promising foal. Yes, she could see the stress lines in his face.

She was sure that's how they'd lured Drew and Willa into the plot — had promised them millions. But Sherry Lynn knew what her son could never know, she understood on a bone-deep level that Riley Hannacker and that woman could not be trusted. Not about anything. Wouldn't do a lick of good to warn Drew about his own father — he wouldn't believe. He just didn't understand, hadn't seen what she had seen, hadn't felt the ripped-open sensation of discovering the lies and betrayal.

"Mom …?"

"What?"

"Are you … your face just flushed … are you feeling—?"

"Fine, fine. I'm fine. Let me be."

She couldn't do that. Couldn't let herself think about it. Couldn't let all the rage out of her soul where she kept it locked away. When she did … you could see it in her. She had to keep the doors locked until …

"I want two things." She looked at Andrea. "I want an Apple Watch like yours." Andrea and Drew both looked surprised. Why on earth would she want a thing like that — she hated everything electronic, didn't even like to use the television remote. But Sherry Lynn had her reasons. She had it all figured out, knew exactly what she had to do.

She turned to Drew. "And I want a dog. Not a puppy, a full-grown dog. Your foreman could help you find one — but I don't want one of those hunting dogs. I'm thinking … maybe a golden retriever."

It was surprisingly hard to keep a straight face as she watched the looks that passed between her son and daughter-in-law. She'd might as well put icing on the cake.

"No party, though. You got to promise. No surprise party."

Drew swallowed. "I promise. No party."

She heard the two of them talking quietly in the kitchen as she sat with her knitting in the den, rocking back and forth. It'd never occurred to Drew when he got her the fancy hearing aids that she could turn them up and hear all kinds of conversations he probably didn't want her to hear. She didn't have to turn them up to know what they were saying, but she listened anyway.

Andrea was saying Sherry Lynn had just had some kind of brain fart this morning and would forget all about the birthday, the watch and the dog by suppertime. Drew was saying he could probably get his hands on a golden retriever, if his mother really did want one. Which she didn't, they both agreed.

She'd bring it up again at supper, breakfast and lunch tomorrow and by suppertime tomorrow night she could work herself up into a snit because they hadn't done as she asked.

Sherry Lynn smiled, kept rocking and knitting, stood way up above that door locked down deep in the pit of her soul where the hatred dwelt. Looked as passive as some poor fool who didn't have all her marbles.

At times like last night when she knew, when she got it,

really *got it,* understood what was going on — at those times she was aware of the fact that something was wrong with her mind. When she was lucid like that, she was aware that fog rolled into her mind — often — and when it did, she couldn't see anything clearly. But she didn't waste that time of clearheadedness to ponder whether or not she was going bonkers. All old people went bonkers eventually, didn't they, nothing new about that. No, she'd used her "clear" time well, thought out a plan, understood that because of her mental issues she might have trouble keeping to the plan, but at least she had one. And she'd remembered it this morning when she woke up, still did. Yeah, she had a plan to ruin their schemes, a plan to get payback, finally, after all these years.

She'd name the dog Dog, she thought; that way she wouldn't forget the beast's name. She hoped they didn't get her one that licked all the time — who wants a face slathered with dog spit? Yes, she'd call it Dog because that was God spelled backwards. And Sherry Lynn intended to descend on those who'd betrayed her with the wrath of God, strike them down, make them pay.

Somebody said revenge was a dish best served cold. Ohhhh, she liked that! Cold as a dead body. That struck her as hysterically funny and she laughed and laughed.

Chapter Twenty-Eight

Okay, so this was ridiculous. Just admit that right up front and be done with it. It was crazy for Ruth to be so obsessed with keeping their Righteous Weed safe that she'd taken to personally standing guard over it.

There it was. No denial.

Did the fact that she wasn't denying the absurdity of what she was doing somehow mitigate that absurdity? The logic being that if she recognized that her behavior was ridiculous, then it wasn't ridiculous anymore.

Now *there* was some convoluted thinking for you. If I do a dumb thing but I know it's a dumb thing then it's not really dumb.

Well, the semantics of it all did, at least, occupy Ruth's mind as she sat there. And she was clearly in need of something to occupy her mind because she was planning to continue sitting here in the dark with nothing to do for … how long? Until morning? That was hours away.

But realistically, which was better — *lying in her bed* awake all night, worrying about somebody breaking into the barn and stealing weed, or *sitting here in the barn* awake all night, to prevent it?

Until a week ago, Ruth hadn't given a moment's thought to the security of the weed they were growing because *nobody* outside the family even knew it existed. Grow weed by the acre and you have to hire workers to care for it, harvest it, dry it and then hand-trim the buds. Workers talk — oh, not to the law, to their sweethearts, wives, grandmothers, somebody. But growing just 250 plants, the four of them — Papa, Ruth, Willa and Drew — could do all the work themselves. They had hauled in the equipment, had set it up, had planted the individual seedlings. Then Willa'd sat on the plants like a mother hen on her nest — nurturing, trimming, watering, fertilizing and sexing, making sure the field wasn't co-ed, plucking out the male plants before they could fertilize the females. It would never occur to anybody in Callison County that the Hannacker family had decided to get back into the weed business. Why now, after four decades? Even if they did, why would they grow all of it in one spot, *indoors* instead of scattering a few plants here and a few plants there in dozens of secluded locations deep in the hollows where nobody could find them? And Land's End? Seriously? The law never did find out forty-five years ago where they'd processed Righteous Weed. Land's End, and crazy, suicidal Malcolm Murdock had skated. There was nothing connecting the historic horse farm to the Cornbread Mafia.

Oh, they all understood that as soon as Baby Bear's Bed started advertising and marketing, the words "Righteous Weed" would eventually trickle back into Callison County. Nothing they could do about that. But nobody local would take the rumors seriously. Their weed crop was safe for the same reason Willie Ray's buried tanker had been safe — because nobody would believe it existed.

Then Damien Coulter had shown up last week — didn't believe for an eye blink that Papa wasn't back in the weed business. As Papa described it, the man had tried to "charm" him into joining forces with CoulterCulture, Inc., and when that didn't work, offered to buy Righteous Weed seed outright.

"He wasn't the kinda fella who'd give up easy ... but he did."

She could tell her father suspected the man was up to something. Though he never said as much, Ruth was sure Papa thought that what Damien Coulter couldn't buy, he might try to steal.

But to steal it, he had to find it. And that was impossible. Totally impossible. Okay, nothing was totally impossible. Improbable, then. Unlikely. Ruth didn't like either one of those words. What if Coulter *did* find where they were growing it — then what?

It was a barn so there were two sets of bay doors, one on the front of the building and one on the back. Both sets were held closed like the doors of a castle — with heavy two-by-twelves set across them in slots. There was a big gasoline-powered generator outside against the wall on the end of the barn, but you had to go outside to crank it because there was no door on the end of the building. There were "people doors" beside the bay doors on both sides. Both were solid core oak doors that locked, and there were only four keys. During the day, someone was always working in the barn — usually Willa, but they all took a turn tending the weed or just babysitting it. But at night ...?

Land's End had as sophisticated a surveillance system as any facility that housed animals valued at hundreds of thousands of dollars. But the lighting, motion detectors and surveillance cameras tied into the screens monitored by the two night watchmen were set up to secure the horse barns. The barn where they were growing weed was on a hillside half a mile from the nearest horse barn. It was "abandoned" there in the brush and encroaching forest.

When they started work in the barn — coming and going from the back that nobody could see, going over the top of the knob and down the trail to Middleton Road on the other side — they'd installed their own security system, a new and improved version of what the Cornbread Mafia had used to protect their processing site years ago. But the basic element of the earlier system had stood the test of time and remained the same — a simple hose alarm, like those used in gas stations back when the "ding" would summon an attendant to fill your tank and wash your windshield. Though not as glitzy and high tech as the rest of the system, it would sound an alarm if a vehicle turned off the highway on the other side of the knob and drove up the road leading to the back of the barn. The movement sensors in the woods were state-of-the-art, but could be triggered by a deer, a raccoon, even a particularly rambunctious squirrel. They blinked off and on, as random as a Joe's Beer Joint sign. The silent triggering of the hose alarm, however, set off a domino effect in the motion sensors, and they would track the movement of whatever had triggered it, beeping an alarm and displaying the position and progress of the intruder on a map that she, Willa, Drew and Papa had on their phones.

Ruth trusted the surveillance system, she really did. But …

Then, on Monday, Willa offered to take over Ruth's marketing calls for a week. She said Ruth looked exhausted; Ruth said that was the pot calling the kettle black. Truth was, they both were exhausted. Their nerves were frayed, the soon-approaching harvest adding its own special sauce of stress. Willa had made the offer to help Ruth out, but the time away from the farm would be good for Willa, too. So Ruth handed over her appointment schedule, Willa headed out for Lansing, Michigan to meet with the owner of a dispensary called Skymint on Cedar Street and Ruth spent the day in the barn, watering and fertilizing and fussing over the leafy green babies.

And when it got late … Ruth just stayed. Why not? She wouldn't sleep if she went home, and she could go home in the morning and shower, then catch catnaps during the day to make up for the lost sleep. She understood that she couldn't stay up all night every night — the Mighty Self-Appointed Guardian of the Weed — until the crop was harvested, dried, cured, sealed in pound blocks for sale and shipped out. But right now, staying set her mind at ease, and that kind of peace was worth some lost sleep.

She listened to music for a while, then clicked on the Audible app and was instantly caught up in the book she was listening to, *Billy Summers* by Stephen King. The main character, a decorated Iraq war vet turned hired killer, was recalling a place he and his platoon called the "Fun House" when her earbuds suddenly fell silent.

What had—?

Her phone was dead. Duh. Phones had a nasty habit of dying when you didn't bother to charge them, which she typically did at night with the charger by her bed. Well, goody. Now, she had nothing to do but sit. That was all guards did anyway, wasn't it? But the sudden mental and physical inactivity was jarring. Without the distraction of sounds and images, Ruth couldn't control where her thoughts went. Her mother's face suddenly appeared in her mind's eye and a wave of unutterable grief washed over her. Tears literally leapt down her cheeks. It'd just been the two of them for all those years … the "two musketeers," while Papa was in prison. Looking back, it made perfect sense that her mother had felt compelled to leave the letter for Ruth after the car wreck. Her mother hadn't sustained life-threatening injuries, though the drunk teenager who slammed into her was killed. Still, lying there in the quiet in a hospital room, thinking about all the "loose ends" in your life … yeah, Ruth could understand how that'd spark a yearning to "get your affairs in order." So she'd written the letter. And she'd dropped the bomb about Ruth's father on Ruth, Drew and Sherry Lynn.

Yeah, *that* had been a watershed moment. Ruth had been waaaay more delighted to learn that Drew was her brother than she had to learn that the man they visited so faithfully in the federal prison in Beckley, West Virginia, was her father. She had always idolized Drew, loved every second she got to spend with him when he came to tend to his foal. She remembered the first time Drew came to the farm after they'd both found out about their shared father. He'd been in the barn when she got home from school that day and she'd gone running there, startled the horse when she stumbled into the stall, breathless. Then she'd felt inexplicably tongue-tied, had finally met Drew's eyes and saw that he was as confused and shell-shocked as she was. She'd thought to wonder then what it must have been like when her mother told him the truth. She never asked her mother about it, but years later she did ask her mother to tell her about the encounter with Drew's mother, Sherry Lynn. Her mother described it so vividly Ruth felt like she'd been a fly on the wall that day.

Chapter Twenty-Nine

Jessica Monaghan keeps telling herself, repeating the words over and over in her head. "I've survived worse. I've survived worse."

She'd lost Davie, watched him waste away for years until …

She'd survived being kidnapped by Jackson McClusky … and killing him.

She'd survived giving birth to Ruth — a brutal two-day labor and breach delivery — with no husband at her side.

She'd survived raising the little girl alone.

So she can survive telling Sherry Lynn Hannacker that her husband, Riley, is Ruth's father.

Jessie has to do it, there's no way out now. She's already told Drew and Ruth. Like that Spanish Captain Hernán Cortés, the conquistador who burned his ships so his men would have to make a home in the new world, she has left herself no "out." She had already had all the arguments with herself, a hundred dozen times. She knows it's the right thing to do, would have to be done someday, and the longer she waits, the more of Sherry Lynn's life she will waste waiting for a husband who is not going to come home from prison to her.

Jessie and Riley had never dreamed Sherry Lynn would be faithful! Why would she be faithful to a husband locked in prison when she hadn't been faithful to him for the ten years of their marriage he was a free man? Sherry Lynn had cheated on Riley with who knew how many men — Jessie knew for certain the names of four of them but there had been countless others. Riley didn't give her a year, told Jessie she'd find another man in less than twelve months, divorce Riley and marry him. But she didn't. Year after year went by, and she went to see him faithfully in prison and as far as Jessie knew, wasn't shacking up with any other man. She had let herself go after Riley was locked up — didn't put on massive weight like she did after Drew was born, but gained maybe twenty pounds, became plump and plain. No reason not to. Jessie finally figured it out — penance. Sherry Lynn Hannacker was a good little Catholic girl and she'd committed mortal sins ... and had been the source of information about the Cornbread Mafia that'd put Riley behind bars. She must have been being faithful in an attempt to atone for that.

Jessie'd called Sherry Lynn last night and asked if she could come by the house, that she has something she needs to talk to her about. Jessie thought long and hard about the best way to tell Sherry Lynn, the best approach, the best place, the best ... of course, there was no best. But though there was no good way, there were bad ways. Sherry Lynn needed to be home. This wasn't a thing you hear and then get into your car and drive away, abiding by the speed limit and all applicable traffic laws.

Stepping up on the porch, Jessie has an irrational urge to run, to get back into her car and—

The door opens and Sherry Lynn is inside, staring curiously at her.

"What are you standing out here for? Forget how to turn a doorknob?"

For a decade, Jessie has opened Sherry Lynn's unlocked front door, put her head inside and cried out, "Yoooo whooo" to announce her arrival.

Then Sherry Lynn must have gotten a good look at Jessie's face because she says, "Hey, something is wrong. Come in. What is it?"

This much at least, Jessie has scripted. She will sit down across from Sherry Lynn, look her in the eye and tell the story, beginning at being in the barn snipping buds off weed plants when rain suddenly hammered down on the roof and she and the other workers decided to call it a day ... it was getting ugly out there. The others left. She stayed behind to put the tools away. The silence. The freight-train sound. The horse trough. She will tell Sherry Lynn about Riley coming to check on her. And what happened after that, explain it, make Sherry Lynn understand that they never meant ...

But when Sherry Lynn takes her arm and begins to guide her into the kitchen to sit down, she can't do it. She stops in her tracks.

"Sherry Lynn ..." Her voice unexpectedly breaks and the look of concern on Sherry Lynn's face makes it that much harder. "There isn't any way to say this, no way for me to make it easier for you to hear. But I have to ... you have a right to know the truth."

A look of apprehension crosses Sherry Lynn's face and for just an instant, Jessie wonders if she suspects what's coming.

"Sherry Lynn ... Ruth's father is ..." Jessie grabs a breath and holds her voice steady. "Sherry Lynn, Riley *is Ruth's father."*

Sherry Lynn makes some kind of sound, a grunt, shakes her head like maybe there's something on the end of her nose she's trying to dislodge.

"What ... what's wrong with you? Why would you say a thing like ... why would you make up a thing—?"

"I'm not making it up. It's the truth. It was ... only one time. *The day the tornado hit the barn where we were working and Riley came to—"*

"Stop ..." Sherry Lynn begins to back away. "Stop saying that—"

"We didn't mean for—"

She puts her hands over her ears.

"Stop it! Stop lying."

"It's not a lie. Why would I lie about—?"

"Shut up!" Sherry Lynn shakes her head again. "You ... and

Riley?" *She is incredulous. "It can't be … he wouldn't—" She only gets that far in denial before slamming into a truth she has always known: Riley doesn't love her. He never did. How many times had Sherry Lynn cried on Jessie's shoulder about how cold and distant he was? For years.*

Jessie watches the pieces seem to come together in Sherry Lynn's head, watches it begin to make sense to her. A horrible, horrible sense. "You … and Riley!" This time, it isn't a question.

"Sherry Lynn, I'm sor—"

Sherry Lynn slaps her. Hard. So hard Jessie's head snaps to the right and a fire lights up her whole cheek.

"You bitch!" Sherry Lynn growls the word in a voice full of pebbles. "You …" Sherry Lynn's rage transforms her face into an unrecognizable mask. "All those years behind my back—"

"No, not years. It wasn't like that. It was just the one—"

"Get out!" She shrieks the words and begins to shove Jessie the few steps back to the door. "Get out of here. Get out of my house. You … you whore!"

She takes another swing at Jessie, but Jessie dodges back, turns and hurries out the door. Sherry Lynn follows her, screaming, poking her in the back, shoving her to make her move faster across the porch and down the steps. She begins shrieking obscenities, her words making no sense. If Jessie hadn't been so much bigger and stronger, Sherry Lynn would have leapt on her. Instead, she balls her hands into fists and begins to beat on Jessie's back before she reaches her truck, pulls the door open and jumps inside. She slams the door in Sherry Lynn's face but Sherry Lynn continues to beat on the closed window, her eyes wild, screaming until spit is flying from her mouth.

Jessie pulls out of the driveway with Sherry Lynn running along beside the pickup, beating on the window. Then Jessie turns and speeds away. The image of Sherry Lynn in the rearview mirror, standing in the middle of the street, shaking her fists … she's sure it will haunt her for the rest of her life. And it does.

Chapter Thirty

Sherry Lynn's hands were so gnarled and twisted by arthritis, with lumps on her finger and knuckle joints that she had once held them out to a doctor and asked why none of it hurt.

"You look at these hands and you'd think I couldn't hold a fork to feed myself." She'd turned them over palm up, wiggled her fingers, made a fist. "They work fine. Why is that?" He had informed her, best she could remember, that arthritis was funny like that — and foisted the horse and chicken platitudes on her — gift horse/uncounted chickens.

She was grateful for the functioning old-lady hands this morning as she fastened the leash to the collar of the golden retriever. Drew and Andrea'd found a good dog, Sherry Lynn had to hand it to them for that. It was a beautiful animal, with silky golden fur and one of those dog faces that sometimes looked like he was smiling. Of course, none of that mattered to Sherry Lynn. She didn't give a rip about dogs, an ugly mutt from the pound would have suited, but she'd asked for a golden because she needed an animal that was at least trained to do the basics — sit, stay, come, all that. Pure-bred goldens were expensive. If you could afford one, you were likely willing to pay somebody to teach it how to behave.

When she'd told Andrea that morning that she intended to take Dog for a test ride, she'd met the expected opposition. But she'd been ready. Holding out her wrist where her birthday Apple watch rode the top of her arm, she'd pointed to the "Find My" apps. There was no sense in having the dog as an excuse to walk around if she was tethered to the house.

"I can't get lost with this tracker thing on my arm," she said. "Might as well be a parolee with an ankle bracelet."

That'd been the point of getting the thing, of course, but she had let Andrea think it was *her* idea to use Sherry Lynn's new watch to make sure she didn't "wander off." They'd never have let her walk the dog out of their sight even on the grounds of Land's End, not after she had "gotten turned around" that time when she was out walking, somehow ended up in the woods by the road. At least that's what they said had happened, though she didn't remember it that way at all. She hadn't been lost. She'd known where she was … she just hadn't known how to get back to the house was all.

The watch, with its tracker app, maps app, telephone and message service was Sherry Lynn's ticket to freedom. And unless she was free to wander the grounds of the horse farm, she would never locate "Willa's garden" where they were growing Righteous Weed.

"Don't go far," Andrea cautioned, as Sherry Lynn and Dog headed out across the back lawn toward the gate in the hedge.

"Three miles," Sherry Lynn snapped. "We're going to

clock three miles today … and we're *not* going to do that in the driveway."

It was a beautiful day and it didn't take long for Sherry Lynn to get hot and winded. She'd get back in shape, wouldn't take long at all. The dog suddenly stopped, hunkered down and crouched in an undignified dog-pooping stance in front of a barn. Sherry Lynn stood patiently waiting for him to finish doing his business. She was quiet, listening to the sounds of workers around her. The stable hands, the trainers, the handlers, the groomers — there were probably three dozen employees.

She smelled dog poop as well as horse poop. Just standing there. Waiting.

For what?

She couldn't remember.

Sherry Lynn looked around, disoriented.

Then out of a shrouding mist, like fog rolling in off some far-off marsh, a man strode toward her. He was tall, black hair in a widow's peak over his forehead.

"Hey, beautiful," he said, and smiled, and she was suddenly aware that she was a mess. Reaching up, she smoothed her long dark hair. Was her makeup smeared?

"Hello, yourself," she purred, and took a step toward him before she pulled up short. Looking down, she saw a dog on the end of a leash she was holding. The dog was taking a dump and she was so embarrassed her cheeks flamed instantly red. The man held out his hand to her, and when she touched him her plain shirt, jeans and running shoes faded into the mist to be replaced by the spike heels she wore whenever she wanted to accentuate her legs.

Just like in the movie *Cinderella*.

"May I have this dance?" he asked.

"Of course," she said, and he took her into his arms,

moving slowly across the dance floor as the band played "Feels Like the First Time." She loved Foreigner. She stumbled, almost tripped over something attached to her arm. Something like a dog leash. She regained her balance as he pulled her closer.

"Can I see you tonight?" he whispered into her ear.

"Of course," she said, "I can't wait—"

And then Steve was gone. There, then not there. Poof.

She was standing in the sunshine, not on a darkened dance floor. But she wasn't sure where she was. She looked around, turned slowly in a circle, taking in barns and people and horses. A dog sat obediently in the dirt in front of her and she saw that the animal was attached to a leash she was holding. She dropped the leash instantly. Whose dog was this? Sherry Lynn couldn't stand dogs, always trying to lick you — disgusting!

And then she was afraid. *They* knew what she was planning, had found out somehow. And they were coming for her. She whimpered in fear, looked around frantically and saw a house, a big white house with a wide lawn and white fence. Maybe she could find help there. Maybe they'd hide her.

She took off running toward the house, dodging a man leading a tall majestic horse out of a barn. She didn't like horses either. They terrified her.

Chapter Thirty-One

Sherry Lynn kept walking, ambling along with her dog leading the way. She used to make fun of that. She'd see somebody walking their dog and the dog was way out in front on a long leash, and she'd think, "Well, wasn't it sweet of that dog to take that man on a walk." Because that was what it was. The dog was taking the human for a walk, not the other way around. She'd always said if she ever had a dog she'd see to it the dog was trained to walk *beside* her. She would decide where they went.

She was glad Dog wasn't trained for that, though, glad he took the lead, because she didn't have any idea where she wanted to go.

Sherry Lynn always knew *why* she was going for a walk when she left the house. Remembered clearly. Knew it was part of her plan. She'd done everything she knew to do to help herself remember. Every night before bed — every night when she remembered to do it — she wrote PRETTY THINGS in lipstick on her mirror above her sink. Then she'd put a big X on top of it. The first time Andrea asked what it meant, Sherry Lynn told her haughtily that she didn't know because she didn't put it there. She was very convincing because she really didn't remember doing it. But then she did and remembered why. Memories were like that — there and then gone and then back again.

But she couldn't manage to hold onto the why this morning. She looked up and noticed she and the dog were walking along the fence line in the front of a horse farm and wondered what on earth she was doing there. She looked around, disoriented, and got frightened. Was this … was it that field where she and her little sister found that baby rabbit and Sherry Lynn had let Annie hold it as they ran back to the house — they'd keep it, make it a pet, play with— But Annie'd squeezed it too tight and by the time …

Bzzzz-bzzz!

Sherry Lynn looked around. What was—?

Buzzz-buzz. Her wrist, the bracelet on her wrist …

Her Apple watch. Andrea's name appeared on the screen and Sherry Lynn tapped the green button and started crying, begging Andrea to come get her.

By the time Andrea came roaring up in her pickup truck, Sherry Lynn had calmed, the fog had washed back out to sea, and she knew where she was and why she was there — taking the dog for a walk as an excuse to search the farm for Willa's garden. It was here somewhere — in the field out behind the north paddock, or the acreage on the other side of the woods by the Barn Number Three. No, she'd already checked there. Maybe in the pastureland that ran down the side of the knob to the creek.

She'd screwed the pooch this time, though. Andrea made her get in the truck and took her back to the house and wouldn't let her go out again. At supper, Drew dropped the bomb.

"I hear you had a little adventure this afternoon and Andrea had to come get you."

Sherry Lynn smiled at him sweetly and held up her wrist.

"She called me on my watch. Remember when I opened the box on Christmas morning and saw it … I told Willa she'd wasted her money because I'd never learn how to use it."

"Andrea said you got lost—"

"I wasn't lost. I knew where I was every minute."

"Got 'turned-around,' then, and you were a long way from the house."

"Not that far, just down by the road."

"Well, that's a long way. From now on, it'd be better — safer — if you kept Dog inside the fence."

Stay in the back yard?

"I will not!"

"The back yard's huge. You can get all the exercise—"

"No, you can't make me. I'm your mother and I'll go walking wherever I please."

"Mom …" Drew said. She hated the patience in his voice and rage swept over her.

"You think I don't know what you're all doing, but I won't let you get away with it."

She glanced over Drew's shoulder and saw her glass china cabinet, the one where she kept her Waterford Crystal. Her favorite piece was a unicorn whose horn had a gold tip and it was real gold. The cabinet was full of broken glass. The unicorn lay in pieces in the center of a shelf, the gold horn nowhere to be seen.

Her eyes filled with sudden tears of loss.

"Why?" she asked Drew, her voice tear-clotted. "Why did you smash it all?"

"Smash *what*, Mom?"

No, not Drew. He hadn't done it.

"It was Jessie! She smashed it."

Drew looked like she'd slapped him. "Mom, we told you … Jessie's dead. She was killed before Christmas. Don't you remember?"

"Of course I remember." She remembered what they'd *said*, but they'd lied. Jessica *Monaghan* was just fine, thank you very much. Drew hadn't smashed her unicorn, *Jessie* had. She didn't want Sherry Lynn to have pretty things so she shattered them all. Anger returned and dried up her tears.

"You tell that witch I'm about to return the favor!"

Oh, no!

She clapped her hand over her mouth in horror. She shouldn't have said that. Drew would tell Jessie, wouldn't realize the danger. Jessie had them all fooled. Nobody but Sherry Lynn had seen the black depths of that witch's soul. If Drew innocently mentioned to Jessie what Sherry'd said, Jessie would come after Sherry Lynn. Jessie would do anything to protect the Righteous Weed that Riley was growing to make them rich.

Sherry Lynn leapt to her feet — upsetting her glass of ice tea and it poured out all over the table — and hurried out of the room. Spotting Drew's phone on the table in the foyer, she snatched it up and put it in her pocket. He couldn't call Jessie and warn her about Sherry Lynn without a phone! Flying up the stairs, she passed by the door to her bedroom but didn't stop. She continued up the stairs to the third floor, ran down the short hall to the bedroom on the end. There were only four rooms on the third floor — a big parlor that rested beneath the widow's walk somebody had added to the historic old carriage house a hundred years ago, a bathroom and the two bedrooms. The bedroom on the end had a door with a real lock!

Andrea first, and then Drew, came to the bedroom door and asked Sherry Lynn to unlock it. She refused, told them she was safe behind the locked door — "Safe from what?" Drew'd asked. He didn't know, couldn't know how much danger she'd be in if Jessie knew Sherry Lynn was determined to destroy her weed. Sherry Lynn went into the bathroom, lifted the ceramic lid off the back of the toilet and dropped Drew's cell phone into the water. That'd keep him from calling Jessie, at least for the time being. Sherry Lynn would stay put, right where she was, where it was safe.

Drew said that if she didn't unlock the door by morning, he would get workers to take the door off the hinges.

Then he and Andrea went back downstairs and left her alone.

The room had that unused smell common to attics, and was as anonymous-looking as a room at Motel 6, where Tom Bodett would leave the light on for you. There were basic toiletries in the bathroom but her toothbrush was downstairs in her own bathroom. So was her night cream. She took care of her skin. If you didn't, you'd look up one day and see some old hag looking back at you from the mirror and wonder where the creature had come from. Her nightgown, robe and slippers were downstairs, too, so she rummaged in the drawers of the dresser and found some old clothes. There was a nightgown — white cotton, floor-length and flowing, with poofy long sleeves, lots of lace and ribbons.

The long sleeves were fine with Sherry Lynn. Andrea kept the air conditioning cranked and the house as cold as a meat locker in the summertime. Though it was stuffy, this bedroom was considerably warmer than her own. But it was late August and it might get too hot later. She'd have to return to her own bedroom if it did, and as she stretched out on the quilt coverlet on the big, oak cannonball bed, she had trouble remembering why she'd decided to sleep here in the first place.

It was something about Jessie and Righteous weed. Then she fell asleep.

Chapter Thirty-Two

Ruth heard a strange clicking sound which she incorporated into the dream she was having as she sat on the cot with her head leaned back against the barn wall. In the dream, the clicking was the sound of beetles, scarabs scuttling across a rock in the desert as the sand blew around them.

Click. Click-click. Click.

Ruth's eyes popped open and the bugs were instantly gone. Good — she hated multi-legged creatures, particularly spiders—

Click-click-click. Clunk.

Ruth froze. Waited. Listened.

It came again, unmistakable in the silence. The sound was coming from the door on the back wall of the barn. She'd locked it. She knew she had. She was certain. The clicking. Was that ... could that have been the sound of *somebody picking the lock?*

Ruth's heart leapt so instantly into her throat, pounding like a herd of stampeding mastodons, that black spots appeared momentarily before her eyes. She reached for the pistol, lying next to her dead cell phone on the table beside the cot, then rose noiselessly to her feet. Without moving the curtain of burlap that appeared to be nothing more than a ragged scrap dangling from the roof joist, she peered out through one of the strategically placed holes. The door opened inward, and she watched like a mouse eying a cobra as the door slid slowly across the dirt.

The area in front of the big bay doors on the back was piled high with what they'd last hauled to the barn and set inside them — bags of fertilizer. Beside the fertilizer was a pile of white grow buckets — the extras and the ones no longer used because the plant that'd been growing in them turned out to be a male — and Willa had yanked it up by the roots and chucked it into the forest.

Who …?

How …?

Ruth didn't know how much of the "code of silence" still held in Callison County — different decade, different *century*, different norms, different rules. Still, even now, in 2022, she couldn't imagine a Callison Countian giving a stranger or the law the time of day. But apparently, word had gotten out.

Somebody had come to snoop. Or to do worse.

When the door was only partially open, a head peeked around it, some guy wearing a wide-brimmed hat, his face too shadowed to be identifiable. He was a big man with broad shoulders who stood for a few moments, looking around, then carefully pushed the door all the way open and slipped into the barn, leaving the door open behind him.

Ruth was absolutely certain that all her efforts at stealth were useless because surely the guy could hear her heart. It was banging away in her chest like a sperm whale in a fish tank. The man had what looked like an empty bag of some kind in his hand, and when he hurried across the open area to the nearest grow tent, it was instantly clear what he intended to do. He'd come to steal a plant, or a stem, or a cola or a cutting — Ruth wasn't completely sure how much of it you had to get away with to be able to grow a marijuana plant on your own.

Her eyes shot to the cabinet on the front wall where the zip-lock bags of seed were locked up safe. If he took those … but, of course, he didn't know there was seed locked in the cabinets. He'd come to take a plant — those were out where anybody could see them.

When he slipped inside the grow tent, Ruth ran down the wall toward the open door. She had no firm plan in her mind. The surveillance equipment — surely the alarm had sounded, even though she hadn't heard it on her dead phone. Still, that left Willa, Papa and Drew. Willa was in Michigan. Papa was at home asleep. She glanced at her watch — three o'clock. Their farm was fifteen minutes away. But Drew! Drew was less than a mile away, down the hill at the carriage house. Surely, he was already rushing here in response to the alarm. She just had to hold the fort until Drew arrived. Hold the *thief* until he arrived. She couldn't let him get away, wouldn't let him steal their weed.

Ruth felt resolve firm her spine even as terror grabbed hold of her chest and threatened to choke her. Resolve … and budding anger. Yeah, anger. She was mad. If this guy thought he could just waltz in here and steal a precious plant of Righteous Weed … well, he had a couple more thinks coming.

Chapter Thirty-Three

Sherry Lynn sat bolt upright in the bed, the little boy's voice ringing in her ears.

"Mommy!"

Drew was having a nightmare again. He'd had them every night since … The room didn't look right. Where was—?

The cry came again and she remembered. She was at her parents' house where she had taken Drew after Nate was killed, because she refused to let her little boy spend another night under that roof.

She raced to the door. It was locked. Her bedroom at her parents' house didn't have a lock on the door.

"Mommy!"

She hurriedly disengaged the lock and ran out into the hallway. This didn't look right. Where were the stairs? Then she spotted them and ran up them to the second-floor bedroom her brother Buster had given up so Drew would have a place to sleep.

The stairs were dark and so was the landing at the top, but she could make out a door and she opened it and—

A warm fragrant breeze tousled her hair in her face and made her floor-length gown flap. The door led outside! Where was Drew? Taking a step out the door, she inhaled the night smells — honeysuckle and damp grass — looked up at the velvet sky where a full moon lit up the world so bright you could have read the ingredients label on a bottle of aspirin.

The scene laid out before her told her instantly where she was. She was standing on the widow's walk high atop the carriage house at Land's End. The view was spectacular. The huge horse barns marched away into the distance, and the line of white fences that surrounded all the paddocks shone bright in the moonlight. To the south, the old Murdock mansion was lit up with the artistic lighting the historical society had added to the establishment, and it twinkled brightly like a huge Christmas tree. The hills to the north behind the rows of horse barns were dark—

Then not dark!

A light suddenly shot out through the darkness, the beacon on a lighthouse. As Sherry Lynn stared at it, transfixed, the little sliver of light elongated and became a rectangle. The golden rectangle sparkled, the bean stretching out from it like honey pouring out of a beehive. It was so bright and rich and pure, it looked like she might have stepped out onto it and walked through the air in the darkness to the source of the light. A path, like the Yellow Brick Road.

Where was the light coming from? There was nothing but woods on that hillside behind the neat row of horse barns. Then she stood very still, stopped breathing.

Actually, there *was* something on that hillside. She'd gone there once years ago to that old horse barn, looking for Riley. It was in that barn where the Cornbread Mafia had processed their marijuana crops when they were still growing it in Callison County.

Where they had *processed Righteous Weed*!

Her heart took up the rhythm of a timpani drum in her chest. People always said that small, petite Sherry Lynn Bennett reminded them of a hummingbird. Her eyes so blue they were almost purple were the color of a hummingbird's wings. And she felt like one now, her heart beating so very fast, her breathing kind of hitching in and out of her chest.

The Cornbread Mafia had processed Righteous Weed in that barn ... was that what they were doing now, was there a crew of people armed with clippers, trimming? They trimmed around the clock, which would explain the light at ... she glanced down at her wrist and at first didn't recognize the big square thing on it — the Apple Watch. It was five minutes until three in the morning.

The light was so bright, like those sodium—

Sherry gasped then, and stopped breathing altogether. Her hand flew to her mouth. That was it! Those were *grow lights* — they were raising Righteous Weed *inside*. She'd been looking for it in a field, but they were growing it indoors, under lights, in that old barn. That was Willa's garden, the one Sherry Lynn had spent half the summer looking for.

She stared without moving, almost hypnotized by the beam of brilliance. And then pretty things began to dance in the glow. A beautiful white egg, covered in the purest diamonds, sparkling and twinkling, each facet of the diamonds catching the light and refracting it. A vase. The one that designer, what was her name? Madeline, yes, Madeline had said it was too colorful, too bright. But Sherry Lynn liked bright, colorful things, and Riley had said she could have *anything she wanted.* That was the bargain they had struck. He would give her a mansion to fill with pretty things ... to take the place of the love he wouldn't give her. He gave his love to ...

Jessie.

Sherry Lynn would be kept busy making her mansion a showpiece where she could flaunt her wealth ... while Riley played bump and tickle with Jessie.

This time was different, though. This time Riley wasn't raising weed to make money to pay for Sherry Lynn's pretty things. He was growing Righteous Weed now so he could buy pretty things for Jessie. So he could give Jessie *anything she wanted.* So he could shower her with diamonds and crystal goblets and Waterford Crystal and Fabergé eggs.

As Sherry Lynn thought the thought, an egg appeared in front of her, right in front of her, floating delicately in the air a few feet from her face. She reached for it, expecting it to vanish, to go poof and leave nothing behind but a little sparkle like a soap bubble. But it was real, solid — she took it in her hand and her eyes filled with tears. She had only this, this one thing, this lone Fabergé egg from all the pretty things she'd purchased. But Jessie would have ...

Oh, no she wouldn't!

The wave of fury that washed over Sherry Lynn literally carried her backward a step. She wouldn't let them have it. She would destroy the weed, she'd — the egg slipped out of her fingers and fell to the floor and shattered, exploding into a million tiny pieces without making a sound.

She stared down at the ruin and felt her teeth clench. Her hands drew up into fists at her side.

"No," she said softly, but it wasn't her voice that spoke. It was the growl of some primeval beast deep in her chest. She whirled around and raced down the stairs.

Chapter Thirty-Four

Running down the side of the barn, Ruth stayed next to the barn wall. She had to get between the man with the bag and the door, freeze him in his tracks, because she didn't think a "stop or I'll shoot" in the quaking voice of a scared woman would stop him if he was running away.

She got to the back of the barn about twenty feet from the door where the man had entered, then crossed the open space, and positioned herself between him and the door. Feet spread wide, knees bent but not locked, two-hand grip with the gun out in front of her, not sighting on the sight, just down the barrel. Just like the firearms instructor in Chicago had taught her. She hoped she looked like Eddie from *Blue Bloods*, the best, in her opinion, of the herd of way-too-pretty-and-sexy-to-be-a-cop women who peopled the ranks of television police departments.

But this wasn't television or a firing range. This was real life. And real live people like Ruth — normal instead of glamorous, people with car payments to make and clothes to pick up at the cleaners and a To Be Watched list of shows on Netflix and Hulu that would encircle the globe at the equator at least twice — those kinds of ordinary people didn't pull the trigger on a gun and put a bullet into the chest of another human being.

Could she do that?

Gratefully, she had no time to ponder the question before the man stepped out of the grow tent with his back to where she was standing, holding a bag that no longer looked empty. And that pissed Ruth Hannacker off. A flash of rage turned her cheeks hot. That was *her* weed he was stealing, *hers*, and he by God was not going to leave here with it.

"Stop right where you are!" she called out, surprised at the power and firmness in her voice.

He didn't stop, just whirled toward where she stood, likely tensing to make a break for the door. Then he saw the gun in her hand.

"Drop the bag." If he'd drop the bag, leave the weed and run away, she'd be satisfied with that.

He did nothing. Didn't try to run, but didn't drop the bag, either.

"You need to turn up the volume on your hearing aid — I said drop the bag."

"And if I don't?"

If this were a vintage Western, John Wayne or Clint Eastwood, instead of a cop show, she would be holding a Colt .45 revolver and at this point you would hear the distinctive clicking sound when she cocked it. But Ruth was holding a Ruger LCP 380, the gun she was licensed to conceal carry, small, light recoil, no cocking.

"You won't shoot me," he said.

"And you know that how?"

"If you do," he turned toward the barn door behind her to the left, "Buster'll blow your brains out."

Ruth snapped her head to the side, and even as she did so, she knew she'd been tricked. She could see in her peripheral vision the thief launch himself at her. She'd allowed her gun arm to follow her head, moved it toward the door when she looked that way. She tried to pull it back toward the thief, but he slammed into her before she had a chance. The two of them went flying backward and landed with a sickening crunch in the dirt with the huge man on top of her. The pistol flew out of her hand and landed in the dirt ten feet away.

The man was like a cat, his movements quick and sure. He produced a knife from somewhere and held it to her throat. And Ruth Hannacker was more frightened than she'd ever been in her life. Cold terror grabbed her gut in a fist and tightened and she couldn't have drawn a breath even if the brute who smelled of beer, cigarettes and old sweat hadn't been crushing her to the floor.

"I oughta cut you," he snarled as he sat slowly up, straddling her. He shoved the knife back down in her face, danced it in front of her eyes. "I oughta——"

"Drop that knife and get up off my daughter," came a cold voice from the doorway. "Or you're gonna find out what two barrels of double-aught buckshot at close range will do to a man's head."

Ruth looked toward the doorway, where Papa stood with a double-barreled shotgun aimed at the man on top of her.

"Bring a knife to a gunfight, son," Papa said, his voice cold, "and you will *lose.* Every. Time."

The man dropped the knife.

"Get up. You'll want to move so slow you couldn't outrun molasses."

As soon as she felt the man's weight lift off her, Ruth rolled to the side and skittered away on her butt until she was out of grabbing range, then got to her knees and her feet and staggered a couple of steps. She stooped and picked up her pistol and cut a wide berth around the man to stand beside her father.

"Who sent you?" Papa asked the man. "Who you working for?"

The man spit in the dirt in defiance and said nothing.

Her father studied the man, calm and patient.

She had held onto her tongue with all her might because she was afraid if she said anything, anything at all, she would start babbling like a blithering idiot or cry or sob or otherwise humiliate herself.

But she couldn't help croaking, "Now what?"

"Depends on our friend here," her father said. "It ain't like we can call the law to report a burglar who tried to steal our illegal weed. We own this one."

Papa took a step toward the man, who had three inches and fifty pounds on him and she could see the big guy flinch back away from his approach. It wasn't all about the shotgun in her father's hands, either. He had a *presence* that commanded respect.

"I ain't gonna ask again. Who's your boss?"

"You won't kill me," the man tried to snarl, but the sound was just a little too high and tentative for that.

"You got that right. I won't kill you." Papa suddenly dropped the barrel of the shotgun down so it was pointed at the man's feet. "But I *will* blow your foot off." He lifted his eyes to the man's face. "And that's what it'll do — this range, it'll blow your foot plum off, won't be nothing left but pieces of bone and muscles and the like dangling. I stood close as I'm standing to you when Willie Ray Taggart blew Jackson McClusky's foot off his leg. He'd a'bled to death in five minutes ... but Jessie put a bullet in his forehead before he had a chance."

He took a step forward and the man took a step back.

"You know who I am?" The look on the man's face said he didn't. "Now that's a pure D shame for sure because if you did, you'd know I ain't bluffing. Pick which leg or I'll pick for you."

"No! Wait. Okay, don't shoot. I'll ... I work for CounterCulture Cannabis."

"That's a company, not a person. I want a name."

"I work in security. A fella named Huggins is my boss."

"Who's his boss?"

"I don't know, the head of the company, I guess."

Riley lifted his eyebrow.

"I said I don't know. They don't tell me stuff like that. I get called in to do a job and I do it."

"He might not a'told you who ordered the job, but you know — don't you."

"No, how would I—?"

"You ain't running with the big dogs so all you can see is paws and assholes — I get that. But you *know* who's out there leading the pack. I want a name."

"I swear, I don't—"

"Pick a foot."

"No, please ... okay, I don't *know* ... but I've heard things before. And this one came down all the way from the top. From Coulter. Damien Coulter."

Her father nodded.

"How'd he find us?"

"I don't know, some ex-boyfriend, drunk or drugged or something, said it was in a barn."

"This barn?"

"No. I been looking for a couple of days."

"How many barns you searched?"

"Half a dozen. Maybe more."

Ruth could see the man struggling to get his mojo back.

"How much they paying you?"

"Enough." He managed to sound surly.

"Oh, I doubt that. Whatever it is, it ain't near enough. How much?"

"Five thousand dollars — two down and the other three when I deliver the goods."

"What's your name?"

The man said nothing.

"You got a driver's license. When I take your wallet to find it, you ain't getting the wallet back."

Maybe the two thousand dollars down payment was in the wallet, because the man instantly spit out his name.

"Hayes. Smitty Hayes."

"Well, Mr. Hayes, I need you to take your keys out of your pocket slow and easy and drop them on the ground and tell me where you left your wheels." He paused. "I can see it on your face, son, that you still think you got a shot here — just an old man and a woman. Know this for a true fact. The only chance you got of a win is to walk outta here on both feet, and right now you are within a gnat's pubic hair of being fitted for a prosthesis."

The man did as directed, dropped the keys and described where he'd left his pickup truck. "Now put your feet together, right side-by-side so's I can get 'em both with one shot."

"No! I'm not gonna—"

"Yes, you are. That's for standin' there marking out in your head the distance between us so first time I get distracted you can jump me."

"I wasn't—"

"You got to the count of one to put them feet together 'fore I blow one of them off and then I won't have to worry about you tryin' to get away."

The man grudgingly lined his Nikes up side by side.

"Pick up his keys," her father told Ruth, "and tie his shoelaces together."

"Tie his—?"

"He's countin' on bein' quicker'n me." To the man, he said, "You think 'cause you got faster reflexes it'll make up for me being way smarter than you are. The young always make that mistake."

Papa looked toward the back bay doors of the barn, took note of the bags of fertilizer and grow buckets piled in front of them and told Ruth to lift the wooden beam out of the slots keeping the *front* bay doors of the barn shut. Then she was to go get the man's truck and drive it to those doors, open them, and drive the vehicle inside.

She had no trouble locating the truck. It wasn't hidden, just parked where he'd left it a hundred yards or so up the trail from the barn. Papa was very specific about where he wanted Ruth to park the man's truck in the barn — directly beneath the big grow light that hung just beyond the last grow tent. Then he told her to get out of the truck, but to leave the front driver's side door open. Obviously, Papa was planning something, but she had no idea what it might be.

Chapter Thirty-Five

Ruth went to stand beside her father after she'd positioned the truck to his satisfaction. He told her to get her phone.

"It's dead." She pointed to where it lay on the table beside the cot. "Didn't think to bring a charger."

"Then how'd you get here before … *'bring* a charger.' Where was you at?"

"Here. In the barn."

"In the …? Then how'd he get the drop on you?"

She wanted to point out that the man had *not* gotten the drop on her, didn't *surprise* her, that she had *captured* him … but that probably didn't count since the guy was preparing to cut her throat when Papa showed up.

Yeah, when Papa showed up. How did Papa get here so fast?

"Never mind. Use my phone. It's in my hip pocket. I want you to make a video."

He gestured for the man — his name was Hayes — to move toward where she'd parked his truck. "Stand by the door," Papa said. Under other circumstances, it would have been comical to watch the big man try to walk with his

196

shoestrings tied together. When he had Hayes in the light like he wanted, Papa backed away a step and told Ruth to back up several steps to the right until he was satisfied she'd get the picture he wanted.

"My daughter here's gonna make a videotape of your confession — which I'm sure some lawyer would say I *coerced*, but ain't no lawyer ever gonna see this so that don't matter." Papa cocked his head to the side. "You do know, doncha, that I could kill you here, bury your body up in the knobs somewhere wouldn't nobody ever find it, take your truck to a chop shop, and before sunrise tomorrow morning every trace you was ever here would be gone. And you … would just *vanish*."

Her father paused, and there was a flat tone to what he said next. You couldn't hear it and not know for absolute certain that he was telling the truth.

"You wouldn't be the first man a Hannacker's ever done that to."

Ruth couldn't tell anymore whether the man was frightened. He'd had time to clamp down on his emotions and put up a gruff exterior. But she saw fear flicker in his eyes then.

"When I tell Ruth to start the video, you gonna say your name and why you came here. You're gonna say who sent you and what for. I 'spect when Mr. Coulter sees it you're gonna be unemployed, but I imagine you'd rather be missing a job than a foot — that right?"

The man didn't answer.

The calm levity left her father's voice and he turned hard as stone between one heartbeat and the next.

"I asked you a question, son."

He gave it a couple of seconds, before he lost the game of chicken.

"Yeah. I'd rather you didn't shoot my foot off."

Ruth held up her father's phone, tapped the telephone icon in the lower right corner, then slid the list of options above the circle from photo to video. When she did, the circle turned red and three sets of zeros separated by colons appeared above the image.

"Get comfortable so the camera don't wobble."

She spread her feet apart and drew her elbows in to her body, making herself a tripod. The image on the screen was the man named Hayes from the waist up. He was facing her, standing a couple of steps away from the open door of his pickup truck.

"Start recording," Papa told Ruth and she touched the red dot. It instantly became a square, the numbers above the image turned red, and seconds began to tick off in the set of zeroes on the right side.

"It's time for your dog and pony show," her father said to the man. He gestured with the twin barrels of his shotgun aimed at the man's feet. "Start talking."

He did.

"My name is Smitty Hayes and I came here tonight to steal some marijuana plants."

"Because ..." her father prompted.

"I was paid to steal them. I work in security for CoulterCulture Cannabis Company and my boss told me ..." He paused and amended. "The job was ordered from the top. Mr. Damien Coulter told my boss to offer me five thousand dollars to come here and steal some plants. I already got the first two thousand. I'm supposed to get paid the rest when I deliver the plants."

"Deliver them where?"

"Sam Huggins, he's my boss, the head of security. I'm supposed to call him when I got the weed and he'll come get it."

Her father stepped closer, stopped beside the open

truck door. He was now inside the frame of the video, could be seen with his shotgun pointed at Hayes's feet. He never took his eyes off Hayes, but talked to the camera.

"I'm sending you this video, Mr. Coulter, to let you know your man failed, and to make sure you understand what's at stake if you send some other stupid bastard on the same fool's errand."

Then he spoke to Hayes.

"Turn around, lean over and grab hold of your truck — like you was on a cop show and I was frisking you."

When suspects on cop shows were asked to do that, they had their feet spread wide apart. This guy's shoes were tied together, which would make him totally off balance.

"What the—?"

"Do it!"

The man turned slowly and laboriously, then reached out and had to fall forward slightly to reach his truck, his right hand gripping the frame where the door was open, his left on the railing of the truck bed.

"Weight on your arms so you can't straighten up and stand," Dad said.

The man shifted slightly so that he was sufficiently off balance to suit her father.

"Face the truck."

Hayes grudging took his gaze off the shotgun, turned his head so he was no longer looking over his right shoulder at her father.

With his back turned, the man couldn't see that her father took his eyes off his aim on the man's feet and turned his full face toward Ruth and the camera. Shifting the shotgun to his left hand, he reached out and took hold of the door of the truck.

Looking right into the camera, his eyes narrowed.

"Like I said, Mr. Coulter, you need to understand what's at stake."

And with a sudden movement so abrupt Ruth couldn't even follow it, her father slammed the pickup door shut!

Hayes shrieked.

And Ruth saw then that all four fingers of his right hand had been smashed between the door and the frame.

Ruth froze, and she recorded perfectly everything that happened after that. Not just with her father's phone in her hand, but with her mind, her soul. The images were burned permanently into her psyche.

The man screaming, shrieking.

Off balance, he crumpled into the truck, scrabbling frantically with his left hand to open the truck door. It didn't have a lift handle. It was a push button, and his left thumb was in the wrong position to operate it.

Only then did she realize that her father had turned to face the camera full on and was still speaking into it.

"… making my point with *maximum* pain and *minimal* damage. *This time.*"

He turned then and opened the truck door and the man fell to the dirt beside it, cradling his right hand, where all four fingers from the middle joint down were smashed flat. Broken, maybe. Or not. Ruth had gotten her thumb smashed in a car door once. It had hurt like hell — she'd had to poke a hole in the nail to let off the pressure of the blood beneath it and the nail had turned black, then fell off. She hadn't broken anything, but it didn't appear Hayes had been so lucky.

Ruth felt dizzy and nauseous, but stood there frozen, while Hayes screamed and her father talked into the camera she was holding.

"It was Ace who taught me that." He hooked his thumb back at the man on his knees cradling his hand, making no effort to stifle his cries as snot and tears ran down his face. "Ace *shot* every one of them Colombians after that battle you thought was such an exciting tale you was hoping you could find one of the bullet holes. *Shot* them. He said *he* did it 'cause he didn't want to bust our cherries. He told us, 'You can't send a proper message unless there's blood.'"

Her father paused, pointed to the sobbing man on his knees. "*That* is so you'll b'lieve I'm serious, that I mean what I say." He leaned close so his face filled up the whole screen. "Come anywhere near my weed or my family again, Coulter, and I will come after you. Not your company — *you*. This is personal. I spent twenty years in a maximum security prison so I ain't civilized. I fight dirty. I know where you live … where your kids go to college … that house you got on Lake Erie where you go to 'get away.'"

He paused and the man who spoke next was somebody Ruth Hannacker didn't know.

"The only woman I ever loved just … is gone now. Dying ain't got no hold whatsoever on me so I am one *dangerous* son of a bitch. If you mess with me and mine, there is absolutely *nothing* I won't do to make you pay."

Snatching the phone out of Ruth's hand, her father stepped toward Hayes, held it close to his brutalized hand. It was bluish purple, misshapen and swelling. The force of the blow had burst the skin open on the index finger and blood was gushing out the tip. The other fingers were flat. The end of the little finger stuck out at a right angle. It had to be broken.

Papa repeated in a dead, emotionless voice that was all the more chilling for its lack of emphasis.

"Absolutely. Nothing."

Chapter Thirty-Six

Sherry Lynn was bent over with her hands on her knees, struggling to catch her breath, heaving air into her lungs in great gulps. The bottom of the white nightgown she'd found in the dresser of the third-floor bedroom in the carriage house was filthy, wet and muddy, and a large piece hung down where she'd caught the fabric on something and ripped it.

Her bare feet were—

She noticed then, the pain. Her feet were so filthy it was impossible to tell, but they were at the very least badly bruised. As the pain spiked up her calves to her thighs in great heartbeat bursts, she realized she must have cut her right foot on something. Scratched it. And her left big toe—

Bright sparkling spots filled the air in front of her as she struggled for breath, grateful for every minute of every one of those fifteen years of three-times-a-week Jazzercise classes. She'd been the instructor, and she'd been good — a natural athlete. She was! She'd been the best cheerleader on the Callison County High School squad.

Sounds echoed around her, crowd noises and whistles.

Push 'em back, push 'em back, waaaaaay back!

She could jump higher than any of the other girls and was the only one who could leap into the air and come down on the ground doing the splits—

Somewhere nearby an engine started, and the bright lights of the football field began to dim and a dark sky — grayish, not velvet black because of the moon — closed over the top of her. She looked down the road, barely visible through the grown-up weeds, and saw an old horse barn. The front bay doors were open. That's where the light was coming from, blazing out in a beam that'd been blocked by the trees surrounding it — but she'd been up high. She'd seen.

And she had come here—

How?

She had walked, run ...

How had she done a thing like tha—?

Well, duh, one foot in front of the other, that's how.

But she remembered none of it, not one step. She had turned in a rage to run down the steps into the parlor on the third floor of the carriage house and in the next instant she was standing here on the road that circled around the back side of the horse barns, and then wandered through the trees up the hill to this barn, set off by itself.

She went another dozen yards or so, where she could see actually see the barn itself, and a pickup truck was backing slowly out of the bay doors. As soon as it had cleared the building, it stopped, slowly turned and drove forward down the road. The truck drove as if in slow motion, as if the driver were balancing a goldfish bowl complete with fish on the top of his head and he was driving carefully not to spill it.

The beam of light she'd followed to the barn began to

grow smaller and she realized somebody was shoving the bay doors closed from the inside. At the same moment, she realized that when the person driving that pickup truck turned on the headlights, he'd see her standing in the middle of the road, her white nightgown blazing. She turned toward the barn and ran to it, then followed the wall to the end and stepped around the corner of the building into the puddle of darkness there. She'd been looking right into the light and now she couldn't see anything in the absolute black at the end of the barn.

The truck's lights suddenly came on, but it still drove agonizingly slowly. She tried to see in the window when it passed near her, but there was just a form hunched over the steering wheel, unrecognizable. The truck followed the road around the end of the barn, where it circled around to the back side before heading off into the woods. She followed along, walking up against the building as the truck went around the end of the barn. Suddenly something black blocked her path, a big box thing snuggled up against the building. When she stepped around it, she jammed her toe into something she hadn't seen on the ground beside it, tripped, and landed on her hands and knees, barely kept from face-planting in the weeds.

Her toe was screaming but she kept her voice from doing the same. The splash of light from the truck's headlights as it turned with the road to head around the back of the building and then out into the woods behind it briefly illuminated what she'd tripped over. It was heavy, full, and she'd knocked it over on its side, but apparently the lid was screwed on tight.

The truck headlights disappeared, and darkness rushed back in around her and Sherry Lynn's mind went blank.

What was she doing in the garage? Robbie'd done it. That little shit. He'd been mowing the lawn and left the gasoline can out where she could trip over it. She opened her mouth to scream, "Robbie, you come put this can back where it—!" Then a chill night breeze blew her hair into her face, chilled her, stuck her wet clothing to her skin and made her shiver.

She was outside. Where …? She hurt everywhere. Her feet were battered, beat up, the toe on her left foot was—

The darkness wasn't absolute. A light was coming from … it was shining around the end of the building, coming from the back side, but not near as bright as the beam that'd shone out the front.

She knew where she was then. And the power of her returning anger animated her limbs. She got to her feet, could hear voices, but couldn't make out what they were saying. Staggering, wanting to cry out from a dozen points of pain in her feet, she made her way to the corner of the building and peeked around it. What she saw froze her soul.

Standing in the light spilling out of an open doorway was Riley. He had aged, was skinny and bent and his hair was white. But the woman standing beside him had not aged. She was still young, as beautiful as she had ever been.

Jessie!

Chapter Thirty-Seven

The man on the floor wasn't screaming anymore, just moaning, cradling his injured hand and rocking slowly back and forth. His cheeks were slathered with tears and his nose was running, making a shiny glaze on his upper lip.

"Where's your cell phone?" Riley asked him.

The man looked at him stupidly, like he didn't understand the question.

"Your phone? Where is it?"

He gestured with his chin toward the truck.

"In the cup holder."

His voice was breathy from pain.

Riley leaned in and retrieved the phone and handed it to Ruth.

"Send that video to his phone," he said, handing her his own phone that he'd snatched out of her hand. He was sure she knew how to send a video. And she did. When she was done, she handed him back the man's phone and her father tossed it onto the passenger seat of the truck.

Riley told Ruth to untie the man's shoelaces and when

she was done, he stepped back a couple of steps and told the guy to stand up.

"This is danged near over. Don't screw it up now."

The warning was unnecessary. The man had no fight left in him. He got slowly to his feet.

"Start the engine for him, Ruthie. Leave the keys in the ignition."

When the motor was running, Riley gestured with the shotgun for the man to get in. He eased himself behind the wheel, had trouble fastening his seatbelt with his left hand, and it'd be clumsy to shift gears.

Before Riley closed the truck door, he told the man, "Don't you ever come back here. I promise you won't live to see another sunrise if you do." The man said nothing, didn't meet Riley's eyes. "Now git. You done wore out your welcome." He slammed the door shut.

The truck started slowly down the road that circled the barn, heading toward the back road out. Riley set his shotgun down on the table beside an unlit lantern and book of matches, and gestured to the chair beside it.

"Sit down before you fall down," he told Ruth.

When she was seated, Riley went to the bay doors she'd opened to pull the truck into the barn and thought as he closed them that the light shining through would have been visible for miles if not for the growth of trees out front. But from the top of the knob on the other side of the valley ... it could be seen from there, he supposed, though he saw no lights to indicate anybody was awake in the handful of houses there. If they were, they'd think a lighthouse had been set down on this knob.

He walked back to where his daughter sat with her hands in her lap, just staring. He wanted to reach out, put his hand on her shoulder or something. But that kind of ... *intimacy* ... it just hadn't happened. He read somewhere that there was like a critical age for things and if you missed it, it would never come easy again. The critical age for … a little girl to climb up into her daddy's lap, or cry out for him when she had a bad dream, or ask him to open a jar of pickles or pin on her prom corsage or … that age passed while he was locked up in a cage and only got to see her twice a month in a visitor's lounge that smelled of disinfectant.

"Let's go," he said. She stood like a robot and he felt like he needed to do something, say something.

"That was ugly. And *you* wasn't likely expecting it."

She looked up at him. "You were?"

"This or something like it, sure." He picked up his shotgun. "That's why I been sleeping in the tack room in barn number three, so I'd be close at hand. 'Parently, you decided to be even closer."

They stepped out the door on the back of the barn into the darkness, the light from behind them painting long black shadows on the ground.

"You knew Damien Coulter would find us? That he'd come—?"

"I hoped we was hid good but with enough money you can find just about anything."

"And you knew if he did, you'd … do *that*."

Riley felt his voice go cold, couldn't help it, though. It was what it was. He was what he was.

"Told you from the git-go something that *seems* harmless can take you where you never woulda gone."

Ruth stood very still for a moment, then turned aside and vomited noisily on the ground beside the door. Riley stood beside her, awkward, didn't know what to do. When it was over, she stood for a moment to catch her breath, then said, "I need to go home." Her voice was trembly.

Riley's phone rang. He pulled it out and they saw Andrea's name on the screen.

"I tried to reach Drew when the alarm sounded and he didn't pick up. Neither did Andrea, but I left messages. I've got prob'ly a dozen texts and messages from Willa, wanting to know what's up." He answered. "'Lo, son."

"Dad, Andrea got up to … she saw she had a voice-mail, and my phone … I can't find it anywhere. Something set off the alarm?"

"Long story. Party's over."

"Then there was … somebody really tried to—"

"We got rid of him."

"*We?*"

"Your sister and I."

Riley didn't know why he'd referred to Ruth as Drew's sister. She was, of course, but Riley'd never hung his hat on it before. He liked it, though. It felt very *family*. And might be the whole family was about to get a whole lot closer — fighting a common enemy had a way of doing that sort of thing.

"You two are *here*?" Drew didn't wait for an answer, just said, "Come on down to the house. I want to hear all about it."

"Me and Ruthie? You sure 'bout that?"

Riley was very aware that Sherry Lynn now lived with Drew and Andrea. He hadn't seen her in years, figured Ruth hadn't spoken to her in decades. And now … porch light on but nobody home … she might not even recognize them, but if she did … not much telling what she might do.

"Mom's asleep, all the way up on the third floor locked in a bedroom."

"You locked—?"

"We didn't lock her *in*. She locked us *out*." He took a

breath. "She's going downhill fast, got lost on the farm today, and when I told her she needed to stay inside the backyard fence, she had a meltdown. She won't hear a thing way up there — I'll put on some coffee."

"In a *pot*, not that stupid Keurig thingy. This ain't a night for coffee that tastes like apple pie or a cherry sundae."

Ruth pulled her keyring out of her pocket and locked the door behind them, then gestured toward her car parked on the other side of his old farm truck. "My rental doesn't smell like manure and my stomach's queasy right now." The two of them got into the Honda, and as Ruth drove around the barn to the front side and down the overgrown road to the house, Riley sent Willa a text.

Chapter Thirty-Eight

Sherry Lynn could only hear their voices as Riley and Jessie stood together in the open doorway of the barn. She couldn't hear what they were saying and she wanted to know. She wanted to listen, eavesdrop, sneak into their lives when they weren't looking and see what it was like there.

Then Jessie turned aside and threw up! She heaved and heaved, splattering puke in the dirt and Sherry Lynn had to clamp her hand over her mouth to keep from bursting out into gleeful laughter. How romantic! She hoped the two lovebirds got vomit all over their shoes.

A giggle did escape her throat then, but she ducked back behind the end of the building and she didn't think they heard. As she hid in the dark, she heard a door close, and then a car engine started and the Honda that'd been parked next to a beat-up old pickup truck behind the barn drove around the building and then down the overgrown road in front of it toward Land's End below.

Now Sherry Lynn was alone, and inside the building she stood beside was "Willa's garden," the weed crop Riley'd planted so he could shower Jessie with diamonds.

Well, that wasn't gonna happen. Sherry Lynn would destroy …

And how, exactly, did she plan to do that?

Until that moment, it hadn't occurred to her how she would destroy their precious weed crop. She only knew she had to do it, figured she'd come up with a way when the time came. Well, the time had come, and she had no way.

Think!

The darkness around her was so absolute it felt like she was a part of it, that her thoughts would float out of her invisible head and she could see them suspended in the air, lit up and glowing like the floating Fabergé eggs.

Shoot, she couldn't even get to the weed. It was locked up tight in the barn. Well, fine, she'd just have to destroy the barn with the weed inside. Drop a bomb on it, blow it up somehow—

Burn it.

The words hung suspended in the air before her, kind of bobbing there, like they were floating on the surface of black water.

Fire.

How could she start a fire—?

Gasoline! She'd tripped over a can of it beside that box thing that was probably a gasoline-powered generator, in case the electricity failed. Wouldn't want those little miniature suns shining down on the weed to go dark! This building was at least 150 years old, maybe older. The lumber that'd been used to construct it was as dry as the end of a matchstick. She'd heard Drew talk about the fire danger in the old barns — which was why he'd begun building pre-fab barns a couple of years ago, moving the horses out of the wooden structures and into fire-safe ones, using the older buildings for storage and equipment.

She hurried to the can she'd tripped over, could see

better now because her eyes were adjusted to the dark. And she found, to her utter delight, that there were *two* cans of gasoline, not just one.

Picking up the first can, she had trouble getting the lid unscrewed, strained and struggled and was just about to give up when the seal broke. She started around the building with it, splashing it up on the boards of the barn. She made it from the generator to the back corner of the building, around it and all the way to the double bay doors where the light had been shining out on the front when she ran out of gasoline. Her arms and back ached, the stink of the gas made her dizzy, nauseous. The liquid she spilled had splashed on the bottom of her gown and on her battered and injured feet. Now they burned like they'd been set on fire. She wasn't at all sure she could splash out another whole gallon.

Losing her focus for a moment, her mind swam and images began to appear in the air before her. The Fabergé egg, the one she'd tried to put in her pocket when she saw it earlier in the night, was there, but it was bigger, the size of a cantaloupe — rubies and emeralds as big as her thumbs, diamonds as big as marbles. She dropped the empty can, stood swaying in the moonlit darkness.

Then Jessie walked up to her out of the darkness, reached out and snatched the egg away.

"Keep your hands off that," Jessie snarled. "That's mine."

Sherry Lynn tried to grab it back from Jessie, but Jessie used her beautifully manicured fingernails to claw at Sherry Lynn's hands, raked deep gouges down her arms.

Sherry Lynn shrieked and Jessie burst into maniacal laughter.

"Riley told me when he sells this weed I can have *anything I want*," Jessie said. "I'm going to buy ten eggs bigger and more expensive than this one—" She turned suddenly and hurled the beautiful egg away into the darkness. It glowed green somehow, and Sherry Lynn saw it hit the ground and roll to a stop in the distance.

She tried to brush past Jessie to go and get it, but Jessie grabbed her arm and snarled into her face. "Don't you touch that, bitch. It's mine, all of it. Riley's mine." She whispered the rest, laughter sparkling in her eyes. "Do you think he went to prison for you? *You?*" She threw her head back and laughed and her blonde curls danced around her face. "You believed that when he told you … promised you'd be a better mother … swore on your love!" She laughed even harder. "He didn't go to prison to keep you free. He went for me, because he loved *me!*"

Sherry Lynn couldn't breathe. The words had knocked all the air out of her lungs. Because it was true. She knew it, had always known deep inside that Riley didn't love her and never had.

"That barn full of weed is going to buy me a mansion bigger and more grand and full of more pretty things than that ugly gauche hovel you built with its ticky-tacky knick-knacks.

Sherry Lynn reached down for the empty gasoline can, intent on smashing it into Jessie's face, lifted it and drew her arm back but Jessie was gone. She could still hear Jessie's laughter, though, like the titter of birds in the trees all around her. Taunting her.

Sherry Lynn would rather die than see Riley and Jessie living in luxury. She forgot about the pain in her arms and back and feet, ran around to the end of the barn for the second can of gasoline to splash on the old wood of the barn walls. Now, she was the one laughing. Laughing so hard she could barely stand and a cloud of fog moved into her mind and covered everything in a blanket of cotton. A single heartbeat later, she was standing again at the end of the building beside the generator, holding an almost-empty gasoline can, but she had no memory of splashing the liquid on the building.

She stood, panting, looking at the deeper black of the barn against the night sky.

Fire.

Now, she would burn it down.

That's when she realized she had nothing to start the fire with.

She turned slowly around in a circle, trying to figure out … how could she start—? Maybe there were matches or a lighter in the barn. She dropped the gasoline can and ran to the door, smelled a whiff of the vomit in the dirt and tried the knob. It was locked. Her eyes fell on the pickup truck parked behind the building. She rushed to it, opened the door and the overhead dome light came on. She dug around in the cab, dumping out the contents of the glove box, searching under the seats. No lighter. She pushed in the cigarette lighter in the dashboard, but it never popped back out.

The keys were dangling in the ignition. Was the key to the locked barn on that ring? Snatching up the keys, she ran back to the barn door. One after another, she tried the keys on the ring in the lock. She was down to the last key … it had to work. She shoved it into the hole, turned it, and the lock clicked open. When she opened the door, the glare of the grow lights blinded her and she squinted and shielded her eyes. The smell of cat piss overwhelmed her. She had always thought marijuana smelled like cat piss.

Somewhere in here, there had to be something she could use to start a fire. Running from one grow tent to the next, she looked inside each, found nothing but big pots with huge marijuana plants.

Panting, she stood near the back bay doors, trying to figure out …

She spotted a table then with a lantern on it. Beside the lantern was a packet of matches. She went to the table and picked up the matches with trembling fingers. Rooster Run General Store was printed on the outside of the package. It was only missing two matches.

Sherry Lynn walked slowly out the door into the night air and turned left. She struck a match, let the flame catch, then tossed it into the spill of gasoline on the back wall of the building.

It didn't catch at first, looked like it was about to fizzle and go out. Then there was a gratifying *whump* sound and she saw a flicker of flame dance on the surface of the wood. The red dancer whirled and spun, and began to move languidly around the base of the building in both directions.

She looked in through the open door at the grow tents and had a horrible thought. What if those didn't burn down? The building would surely go up like a torch, but maybe the plants inside the grow tents would be spared.

That wouldn't do. She looked around, spotted the almost-empty gasoline can she'd dropped, and took it inside to splash gasoline on the tents themselves. Up and down the rows of white tents she went, ten feet by ten feet, in neat rows. Smoke was pouring into the building from the burning walls. There was only a little gasoline left in the can. She bent, picked up a piece of fabric torn from one of the tents and soaked it in the remaining gasoline. Stepping away from the tents and the gas can, she struck a match, and lit the piece of fabric.

She tossed the flaming fabric at the nearest tent and heard the satisfying whump sound as the fire caught. She turned toward the barn door. When had the barn filled with smoke? It was so thick she could barely see and suddenly she was coughing, couldn't breathe. Then she saw the gasoline-soaked piece of tent fabric dancing on its own, the red-orange flames rising up into the air, watched as the colorful flames followed the dripped gasoline back toward where she stood.

Then a tiny tongue of flame kissed the edge of her gasoline-soaked nightgown. She lurched away and began to scream.

Chapter Thirty-Nine

Ruth sat in Drew's kitchen drinking coffee so strong and thick you could trot a mouse across the top. She was trembling inside, could feel the shake deep in the marrow of her bones, but the shakes didn't make it all the way to the surface and her hands were steady. Her father was seated at the end of the table facing the kitchen window with Ruth on the left and Andrea and Drew on the right — both dressed in bathrobes, looking bleary-eyed, trying to take it all in.

Ruth had never been in the carriage house. She'd been fourteen when Willa was born, and at that time Drew and Andrea were living in a tiny apartment in Lexington, close to Calumet Farm, the seven-hundred-acre thoroughbred breeding farm where Drew had just gotten his first job.

She'd been a freshman at Stanford when her father was released from prison and she spent the following summer at home in Callison County ... she and her mother and father learning how to be together as a family. After that, she never lived at home again — spent a summer studying in Italy, then was busy launching her businesses, struggling to make a success of herself in what was, even then, mostly a man's world.

Since she'd been home, she saw Drew often when he came to meet with her father and Willa at the farm. She'd never come here, though, for the obvious reason that one of the people who now lived here would not have welcomed her presence. In fact, Ruth looked up now and then, into the puddles of shadows in the dining room she couldn't see and the other rooms beyond it. As she understood it, Sherry Lynn was no longer in possession of all her marbles, and seemed to be losing more and more of them every day. Ruth had seen the woman often in those days before her mother's car accident. Sherry Lynn would bring Drew over to play with his foal, and then she and Mom would sit out on the porch in rockers, shelling peas or maybe husking corn. Her memories of the woman were vague — and she never laid eyes on her again, not even at a distance, after age nine. What she remembered most were the voices of the women on the porch — her mother, calm and soothing, usually placating because Sherry Lynn was always whining about something. If you'd asked her at the time, and of course, nobody ever did, she'd have said she did not like Sherry Lynn Hannacker.

Oh, how she hoped the woman didn't suddenly materialize out of the shadows in the doorway, the Ghost of Christmas Past, and want to know what was going on. She cast a fearful glance in that direction, then pulled her attention back to the conversation.

Willa had called as soon as she got her grandfather's text, had been absolutely frantic when she couldn't reach any of the other three after the intruder alarm app went off on her phone. She'd been minutes away from getting into her car and starting the five-hour drive from Michigan back to Kentucky.

Papa set his phone down on the table and put it on speaker so Willa could hear and participate in the conversation. Ruth's father didn't pull any punches, told the story just like it'd happened. All of it.

When he described the incident with the car door, Andrea put her hands over her mouth. Her eyes were huge, but she said nothing.

Everyone was quiet when he'd finished the story until Drew dropped words into the puddle of silence.

"How'd he find the weed?"

Ruth's stomach lurched and she was afraid she was about to be sick again. But the look on her father's face … he didn't want to have to say it, so she did.

"He said they drugged … an *ex-boyfriend*."

They could hear the sound of Willa gasp out the speaker.

"Ex-boyfriend?" Her voice was airless. "But I didn't … I never told Isaiah—"

"Just the barn part," Papa said. "He searched a whole bunch of others."

"Oh." Willa's voice was a barely audible whisper. "Oh, no …"

"*Drugged,*" Papa said. "*Whoever it was* didn't say nothing on purpose."

The sounds of Willa's muffled sobs came through the speaker and yanked at the heartstrings of every person seated at the table.

"You think you scared Coulter off?" Drew asked, clearly determined to drag the conversation in a different direction. Ruth cast another glance at the darkened doorway leading into the dining room and Andrea saw.

"I'll go upstairs and check on Mom," she said, got up and left the room, grateful for an excuse to bow out of the upsetting conversation.

"I hope we scared him," Dad said. "Coulter struck me as all hat and no cattle."

When Drew raised his eyebrows, Papa described his impressions of the man, how he didn't trust—

He stopped when Andrea reappeared in the doorway.

"Mom's not in the bedroom. She's gone. The door's unlocked and standing open." She sighed and looked balefully at Drew. "Guess we better start searching the house." She shook her head. "No telling where she's decided to sleep."

"Payback." Papa turned to Ruth. "Maybe you'd call it karma. When Drew was a little boy, he'd get up in the middle of the night and we'd find him the next morning asleep under ..."

His words trailed off and she saw his focus shift from her face to some spot over her right shoulder. Confusion knit his brows together, then recognition shot both eyes open and they stared like saucers.

They all turned to look out the window. "What ...?" Drew began. A red light was flickering against the window-pane, and when Ruth looked through it to the source, she couldn't at first figure out what—

"Fire!" her father cried. "The son of a bitch came back and set the barn on fire."

Papa leapt to his feet and started for the back door, with Ruth one step behind him.

"You're not coming with me," he snapped.

"The hell I'm not!" She held up her car keys and brushed past him and out the door.

"I'll call Buster," Drew said.

Land's End had its own firefighting equipment. Of course it did — horses worth hundreds of thousands of dollars in barns full of hay! Buster Lockridge was the night foreman and he'd call out the troops, though the old barn on the hillside was too remote to be a danger to the barns where the horses were housed.

"Get somebody out front to stop the fire department if someone sees the fire and reports it," Papa called over his shoulder. "Tell 'em we got this."

Wouldn't do for Callison County volunteer firemen to come rolling in on a pumper truck and see what was inside the burning barn.

They had to get that fire out *quick*!

Chapter Forty

They were only halfway up the road to the barn but it was already clear to Riley that "getting the fire out quick" was not an option.

There was also no need to worry about what Callison County firemen might see inside the barn if they showed up to put out the blaze. By the time they arrived, there'd be nothing left inside the barn to see.

It was a flaming torch on the hillside, with a ring of fire on the lower part of the building all the way around it — the flames eating into the dry boards above as ravenously as chainsaws.

It'd be long over before anybody arrived to help.

Ruth pulled the car to a screeching stop behind the building, where they saw the door they'd locked behind them standing wide open. The view inside was boiling flames. It looked like hell had opened up a crack in the world right there in that barn. The two of them leapt out, stood gaping in horror for maybe five seconds.

Then they heard screaming.

Ruth turned to him, the light of the flames dancing on

her cheeks. She said something. He read her lips — *some-one's in there!* — but didn't hear the words. Not because they weren't loud enough but because a roaring, rumbling sound had suddenly filled his head, a somehow familiar roar that was way louder than the thunder of the fire.

More screams. Wailing.

Not a man's voice. It wasn't the guy whose fingers Riley had smashed in a car door, come back to destroy what he hadn't been able to steal.

It was a woman, her shrieks a filleting knife that sliced Riley's soul in two.

The rumbling in his head sounded like gravel in a blender, echoing behind his eyes, bouncing off the insides of his skull, a wrecking ball of sound crashing into his mind. He recognized the sound then. He'd heard that freight-train rumble before.

Standing with only one boot on in a shower in Vietnam, watching naked Cong soldiers slither through the mud.

Walking toward the barn behind the house, the dirt turned to quicksand trying to suck him down, the look of ragged grief on LeRoy Taggart's face.

Clutching Jessie to his chest in the dark as the world exploded around them, rain pelting them in their own living room, the wind pulling Jessie out of his grasp.

Reality stopped. Time stopped. The earth stopped spinning, locked in place, fixed at some solid point in space in its orbit around the sun as Andrea's voice whispered softly into his ear: *Mom's not in the bedroom. She's gone. The door's unlocked and standing open.*

Sherry Lynn wasn't asleep in some odd place in the carriage house, maybe beneath the dining room table — Drew's favorite spot — or in the recliner in the living room. Sherry Lynn was here — in *there*!

It seemed that the realization, the assessment of what his ears were hearing, took a lifetime. Sherry Lynn had come here, set fire to the building, then got caught inside.

His understanding of what that meant took an eon.

His decision to act took a millennium — all of it compacted between one heartbeat and the next.

When Riley started to run toward the building, Ruth grabbed his arm.

"What are you doing? You can't go in there!"

"That's Sherry Lynn."

Her face registered shock and disbelief. She hadn't recognized the voice.

"No, it …"

He tried to shake off her grip but she held fast.

"Papa, no! You can't get her out. It's too late."

"I have to try." He didn't know it was so until he heard his own words confirm the truth out loud. He did have to try. He couldn't have explained why even to himself because the reasons were as tangled up as a ball of twine in his chest. *"I owe her!"*

Those three words untangled all the twine into a single long, straight line. He owed Sherry Lynn because he should have told her when he returned from Vietnam that he'd been planning to break up with her. He should never have married her. Drew was entitled to a father, but a woman who'd seduced him into one act of sex was not *entitled* to a husband. He'd done the easy thing, and made them both miserable. Sherry Lynn *had* been entitled to a husband who did love her, and if Riley hadn't been too cowardly to do the right thing, she would have found that man. Mostly, he owed her for the gigantic lie he'd told her the day before he was shipped off to prison. He'd said then he *did* love her, that he was proving it by taking her place in prison. He'd said that in a last-ditch attempt, a Hail-Mary effort to make Sherry Lynn release her stranglehold on their son and allow him to grow up normal. It'd mostly worked, so it was hard to be sorry for it. But the lie had kept Sherry Lynn waiting for him for a decade. For ten long years, Sherry Lynn was the loyal wife, waiting for her loving husband to be released from prison. It was all a sham. Jessie'd ended it by telling Sherry Lynn the truth — telling them all the truth — the day after Drew graduated from high school. And Sherry Lynn had made her rage at that betrayal the centerpiece of her life, and everything she did in the decades afterward could be traced back to it. Three more husbands, one after another — Tim Brand, Benjamin Connelly, Clive McClusky — like they were on an assembly line. Her hate ate her soul.

Yep, the ruination of the life of Sherry Lynn Bennett Hannacker Brand Connelly McClusky could be laid at the feet of Riley Hannacker.

He owed her!

Wrenching his arm out of Ruth's grasp he raced toward the open door. Ruth's screams — "No, Papa, *noooo!*" joined Sherry Lynn's screams of terror to form a shrieking cacophony in his head. Flames were everywhere — not just the building, but the grow tents inside it. He took two steps into the smoke-filled interior of the building, his eyes straining to see where …

He spotted her then. She was running toward him — trying to outrun the flames eating up the length of her white nightgown. He raced to intercept her — got a clear look at the terror and pain on her face, then tackled her, rolling her over and over, trying to put out the flames in the fabric.

There was a gasping moment then, a frozen moment. He lay on top of her. Her nightgown was out, but the smoke was now so thick … so very thick. Recognition replaced the terror in her eyes. Sherry Lynn's lips formed a word — *"Riley?"* Then there was a great, rumbling roar all around them. He looked up, saw blazing timbers crashing down out of the ceiling.

Then the world went black.

Chapter Forty-One

The smell of flowers in the living room of the carriage house, arrangements brought back from the funeral home, gave way to the aroma of chicken — fried, broiled, baked, casseroled, barbecued or salad-ed — in the kitchen. That was just the various varieties of chicken, but that was not all — oh, no, that was not all. Ruth had the image of Dr. Seuss's Cat in the Hat driving some Rube Goldberg machine through the house depositing various edible dishes on every available surface up to and including the toilet bowl tank in the bathroom.

"There's enough food in this house to feed all the blond men in the Norwegian army," Willa whispered under her breath to Ruth.

"We oughta donate it to a homeless shelter."

Willa merely raised an eyebrow.

"Okay, no homeless people in Brewster. My bad."

Andrea and Drew were ushering the stragglers toward the door, finally draining the house of all the people who'd come to offer their condolences. What a nightmare.

Ruth looked around and supposed maybe the other family members had been comforted by the herd of people who showed up as soon as they heard about the tragedy and then — there must have been a signup sheet somewhere to ensure the "grieving family" wasn't left alone for a millisecond for four whole days.

Ruth Hannacker had long been of the opinion that the death rites of civilized society were mostly clumsy, antiquated and outdated, and in her experience, usually made the whole situation more difficult to bear. Her mother's funeral had been right before Christmas and Ruth had wanted nothing more than privacy, had been so grateful to escape to her Chicago apartment with its view of the lake — if you stood on a chair and peered out the top six inches of the bathroom window. Okay, full disclosure: as soon as she was alone, she proceeded to fill up about every waking moment with activity in order to *avoid* the privacy that she'd rushed home to find, the alone time that would make it possible/necessary to experience her grief.

She hadn't returned to Callison County until March, when Willa begged her to come home to go through her mother's things, said Papa was mostly a non-functioning zombie and Willa didn't feel comfortable doing it herself.

So Ruth had come. And found the letter. And …

Words floated to her from the departing mourners.

"… such a lovely service …"

"… a good job with the homily …"

"… the right thing to separate the services."

It had been obvious to the rest of the family as soon as they recovered from the initial shock of the deadly fire that they should not have a single service for both Riley Hannacker and Sherry Lynn McClusky. They'd shared a son, but nothing else in more than forty years and it would be macabre to conduct a joint funeral — closed caskets, of course. The funeral director, the soul of discretion, had set up separate viewing rooms in his facility. They'd both been buried in the St. Augustine Church cemetery, of course — Sherry Lynn in a plot next to her last husband, Clive McClusky, and Riley in the plot beside Jessie, next to the Monaghan plots where Davie and his mother Ruth rested.

Sherry Lynn's service had been yesterday, and Ruth had vacillated back and forth about whether she should attend. She loved her brother and his children and wanted to be there to support them, but she was keenly aware that Sherry Lynn would *not* want her there, would be horrified at the thought of being in the same church as Jessie and Riley's daughter, Ruth. She couldn't guess how many of the relatives from Sherry Lynn's previous marriages — ex-husbands, ex-stepchildren, and their assorted families would be there, but she was completely certain that every one of them had gotten an earful from Sherry Lynn over the years about Ruth and her mother and standing around making nice with them sounded like a recipe for awk-ward. Drew'd saved her. Ever thoughtful, empathetic Drew, told her he understood — if it made her uncomfortable, she should not come. It did, and so she didn't.

Her father's funeral had been this morning. Now, as sunset painted the sky above the knobs crimson and gold, every member of the family was emotionally wrung out, running on fumes.

Just go, she had silently pleaded with the throng of mourners and finally, *finally*, they had complied.

Andrea closed the door behind the last of them, and literally leaned against it in relief.

"By official decree from the High Court of What's Happnin' Now," Willa called out as she gently shoved Ruth and her father and mother into the den, "it is ordered that the Hannackers kick shoes off and plant backsides on cushions while I bring all of you a glass of brandy."

Willa's brother-in-law, Joel, had snatched up her younger sister Lissa more than an hour ago, determined to take her home and put her to bed. She did not look good. Such a gentle, simple soul, Lissa had been pale and hollow-eyed at the services. The sudden deaths of both her grandparents had been staggering emotional blows and everyone in the family'd been thinking the same thing — she could go into labor and have the baby early. It wasn't due until the first of October.

Ruth sat down heavily in the big overstuffed chair, watched Drew and Andrea collapse together on the couch. Ruth had lost her father, but Drew had lost his mother *and* father to the fire that had leveled the old barn and destroyed everything that'd been inside — all the plants, the equipment and the seed. It was a wonder Drew was holding it together at all.

Willa sailed into the room with a tray and deposited drinks in front of everyone, then she plopped down in the big brown chair in front of the fireplace. When she leaned back and draped her legs over the arm of the chair, Ruth was transported back to that morning in April when she'd opened Pandora's Box.

They all sat quiet, sipping their drinks, prisoners of their own thoughts.

~

DREW HANNACKER WAS NUMB. Finally, blessedly numb. The silence in the room was such a relief he wanted to wrap it around him like a blanket and drift off to sleep.

Except he wasn't sleepy, just wrung out. And probably to some degree still in shock and denial. He understood that the reality, the finality of what happened hadn't really soaked all the way in. Not yet. It would come at him later, sucker-punch him when he wasn't expecting it — like putting on a tie before his mother's service yesterday and remembering the Christmas she'd gotten it for him. He'd gone into the bathroom and turned on the shower to cover up the sound of his sobs — because he couldn't let it all out then and if Andrea'd heard him, her comfort would somehow have been more than he could stand.

He didn't feel like crying now, though. Just … numb.

Tomorrow, he'd get up and have to face anew the reality of never seeing his father or mother again. Along with the attendant harsh realities of what the fire would mean to the rest of his life.

His eye fell on his sister. Her face in the slanted late afternoon light looked so much like her mother. His father mentioned that often, but Drew had never seen the resemblance as profoundly as he did at this moment.

"Will you be staying long?" he asked her. "It's good to have you around."

"I haven't worn out my welcome?"

"Never."

She let out a long sigh.

"I'm afraid I have …" she smiled ruefully, "promises to keep and miles to go before I sleep."

"Promises?"

She barked out a laugh.

"The miles to go part, yeah. The promises part, not so much. I promised my creditors I'd pay them and that ain't happnin'." She shook her head. "I will, however, be keeping a promise to my lead attorney. I said I'd call when I'd decided it was time to file the bankruptcy papers for

Has-Beens and Ruth's Stuff. I have decided to keep one store from both corporations, shut down the others — lower the overhead. I figure ditching the rest will give me the time and focus … so maybe I can bring forth a phoenix out of the ashes, or something like that."

She barked out a not-laugh.

"Mr. Ira Broganstein is in for a shock. The last time he heard from me, I told him to start making arrangements to pay off all my creditors *and* all my bank loans."

She glanced at Willa.

"He wanted to know if I'd found a buried treasure."

Willa straightened up in the chair. "About that … the Tree House …"

"Yeah, it seems a shame to leave it just sitting there empty. Oughta be good for something, maybe store winter clothes there to save money on mothballs."

Willa suddenly looked uncomfortable. She opened her mouth to speak, then closed it again.

"'Sup, sweet pea?" Drew asked his daughter.

"I just … well, actually there is something we could do with it."

"It what?" Ruth asked.

"It, the Tree House. I mean, it's just right there, wouldn't have to take it anywhere."

"Take it anywhere? Is that 'it' a different 'it' than the Tree House 'it'?"

"I was just thinking you could use the Tree House to trim marijuana buds."

"Huh?" Ruth asked. "Way out there, hard to get to, hard to get into, small and dark … what about all that would make it a good place to trim buds?

"Proximity."

"To what?"

"The marijuana."

"There's no marijuana near the Tree House," Drew said.

Willa let out a breath and seemed to square her shoulders.

"Actually, Dad, yes, there is."

Chapter Forty-Two

Under other circumstances, the looks on their faces would
have been comical. Nothing humorous now, though, and
Willa wondered if now'd been the right time to tell them,
with their pain and grief still so raw.

"It was an accident," she blurted out.

Ruth sat her glass down carefully on the table in front
of her.

"Accident?" her father said, his voice airless.

"There are four marijuana plants growing around the
rock pile by the Tree House. I've been taking care of them
… as an experiment."

You could have heard a mouse in house shoes tiptoeing
across a cotton ball in the silence that followed.

"Start at the beginning," Ruth said slowly, her eyes
bright, her voice trembly.

"The day we loaded up the money and the seeds — big
storm, remember?"

Ruth nodded.

"Do you remember that I spilled a few seeds on the

floor when I was pouring them from the jars into the zip-lock bags?"

Ruth looked blank.

"Well, I did, and I scooped them up and stuffed them into my jacket pocket. And when we were climbing down off the rocks, I slipped in the mud and busted my ass. Remember?"

Ruth looked like she did remember that part.

"That must have been when it happened. When I fell, some of the seeds dropped out of my pocket into the mud."

All eyes were fixed on Willa.

"I forgot all about the seeds in my pocket." She held up her hand to forestall the question she could see coming. "No, I've washed and dried that jacket three or four times since then — they're gone now. *But* ... sometime in the middle of June, I was going over Willie Ray's ledgers, tracing how he'd come up with different strains, and there was a hole, a gap in the lineage. He'd been so meticulous, and then ... the entries about one hybrid stopped and on the next page, there were entries about a much later strain, starting in mid-sentence. Then it hit me." She slapped her forehead. "Duh, moron. There's a page missing. I thought maybe it had come out in the Tree House, maybe fell behind the shelf where the ledgers were stacked. So I went back to check."

"Did you find it?" Andrea asked.

"Nope. Got down on my hands and knees with a flashlight, looked everywhere, nothing. So I left, climbed up out of the pile of rocks ..." She grinned, remembering the moment. "And there it was, plain as day. I don't know why I didn't notice it when I came up the hill. There was a marijuana plant growing among the weeds at the base of the rocks. I was flabbergasted, thought I was imagining it. I examined it, and it was the real deal. And when I looked around, I found three others. They were small — not manicured and pristine like the ones in the barn. They'd been fighting for survival among the other weeds and undergrowth — skinny and malnourished."

She paused, could see the cogs turning frantically in everyone's heads.

"So I decided to conduct an experiment. We grew our crop indoors to take care of it and hide it and all that, but also because common wisdom is that outside weed isn't as good as inside. I thought — hey, here's some weed growing outside, the same weed we've got under grow lights in the barn. Let's see how much difference it makes. So I cleared out all the weeds and brushed around them, fertilized them — went out there and watered them during that dry spell. I did everything I could to make them strong and healthy. I figured after we harvested the crop, our crop, I'd surprise you guys with the buds from the outside weed and we could compare the yield."

When she finished her story, nobody said anything, they just looked at her and then at each other.

"Okay, let's back this wagon up to the barn and load it all over again," Drew said. He smiled. "Papa used to say that all the time. Let me make sure I'm hearing—"

Ruth interrupted. "You're telling us there are four Righteous Weed plants still alive?"

"That's what I'm telling you. *And* … one of them's a male and I didn't go out there often enough to catch it in time so it fertilized the females. I was bummed when I found it because I wouldn't be able to make an apples-to-apples comparison — *outside* sinsemilla to *inside* sinsemilla, but now …"

"Now, there will be seeds," her father finished for her.

She nodded, took a breath and dropped words into the surprised silence that followed.

"Now, we have to decide what to do with them."

"Do with them?" Ruth was incredulous.

"We can harvest them when they're ready — it won't be long now — and see if Righteous Weed is still … righteous. Off four plants — fertilized plants so they're not as bushy, a lot taller than the ones in the pots — we might get a pound, maybe a pound and a half we could sell. We collect the seeds and grow a second generation and … we're back in business."

"You have a Plan B, though, don't you?" It was her father again. She could tell he was a step ahead of her.

She nodded.

"Plan B is … we destroy the plants."

"Destroy them?" Ruth was incredulous. "Why on earth would we—"

"Because we just buried your father and both my grandparents!"

She hadn't meant to blurt it out that way, sounding so harsh.

"What does that have to do with—?"

"It has everything to do with it. It's what growing marijuana has done to this family." She paused, then continued softly, "And that's not all it's done."

Isaiah had called, had heard what happened to her grandparents, told her he was sorry. She wanted to be furious at him — he *had* to be the "ex-boyfriend" who was drugged by Damien Coulter. But she said nothing about that, was just glad to hear his voice. He'd sounded glad to hear hers, too.

"Ruth, you weren't itching to run a cannabis company.

You weren't all like — 'Hey, I can't wait to ditch the businesses I created, nurtured and grew so I can throw myself into something I neither understand nor enjoy.' It was all about the *money*."

She looked at the soot-blackened walls of the fireplace where no flames danced on logs.

"I just got to wondering … what could I *buy*, what *thing* could I hold in my hand that would mean as much to me as what … what's *gone*?"

They all were quiet.

"Papa said …" Ruth stopped and got her voice under control. "He warned us. Tried to, anyway. I know what he meant now—"

"*Money* is the Tar Baby," Drew finished for her.

"I don't think they saw it coming," Willa said. "Grandpa, Willie Ray and Jessie — they never intended … it all just sort of happened to them."

"And changed them," Ruth said. "Papa … that night in the barn when he … he was somebody I didn't know."

"We're Hannackers, the fifth, sixth — who knows what generation." Willa looked pointedly at each one of them in turn. "And here we are, after all these years, still living like *moonshiners*."

The word hung out there in the air like a dead fish on a stick.

Ruth cleared her throat. "All right, then, we get a license *first*," she said. "We wait until we have a license — then grow enough to get a patent. After that …"

"So you're saying … we *go for it*?" Willa asked. "Stand on the edge of the cliff and jump off … *again*?"

No one spoke for a long moment, and in that silence Willa could feel Grandpa's presence in the room.

"This time the Hannacker family won't hit the rocks at

the bottom," Drew said, and his eyes filled with tears. Maybe he sensed his father's presence, too. "Not this time. This time ... when the Hannackers step off the cliff, we'll *fly*."

THE END

Kidnapping. Murder. Grass-roots justice.

When her father is shot down on the street in front of his office, college journalism professor Sarabeth Bingham abandons academia to take over the weekly newspaper he left behind.

Get Homegrown today.

A Note from the Author

Thank you for reading *So Shall The Tree Grow*.

If you enjoyed this book, please consider writing a review on your favorite bookselling site so other readers might enjoy it too. Just a couple of sentences would mean a lot to me.

Thank you!

Ninie Hammon

About the Author

Ninie Hammon (rhymes with shiny, not skinny) grew up in Muleshoe, Texas, got a BA in English and theatre from Texas Tech University and snagged a job as a newspaper reporter. She didn't know a thing about journalism, but her editor said if she could write he could teach her the rest of it and if she couldn't write the rest of it didn't matter. She hung in there for a 25-year career as a journalist. As soon as she figured out that making up the facts was a whole lot more fun than reporting them, she turned to fiction and never looked back.

Ninie now writes suspense--every flavor except pistachio: psychological suspense, inspirational suspense, suspense thrillers, paranormal suspense, suspense mysteries.

In every book she keeps this promise to her Loyal Reader: "I will tell you a story in a distinctive voice you'll always recognize, about people as ordinary as you are--people who have been slammed by something they didn't sign on for, and now they must fight for their lives. Then smack in the middle of their everyday worlds, those people encounter the unexplainable--and it's always the game-changer."

Also By Ninie Hammon

Cornbread Mafia

Fire In The Hole

Blown' Up A Storm

Ridin' For A Fall

So Shall The Tree Grow

Nowhere, USA

The Jabberwock

Mad Dog

Trapped

The Hanging Judge

The Witch of Gideon

Blown Away

Nowhere People

Through The Canvas Series

Black Water

Red Web

Gold Promise

Blue Tears

The Taken Saga

The Taken

The Changed

The Hidden

The Saved

The Unexplainable Collection

Five Days in May

Black Sunshine

The Based on True Stories Collection

Home Grown

Sudan

When Butterflies Cry

The Knowing Series

The Knowing

The Deceiving

The Reckoning

The Fault

Stand-alone Psychological Thrillers

The Memory Closet

The Last Safe Place

The Gap